Some Truth Can Be Distorted

JANE BLYTHE

Acknowledgments

I'd like to thank everyone who played a part in bringing this story to life. Particularly my mom who is always there to share her thoughts and opinions with me. My wonderful cover designer Amy who did an amazing job with this stunning cover. My fabulous editor Lisa for all the hard work she puts into polishing my work. My awesome team, Sophie, Robyn, and Clayr, without your help I'd never be able to run my street team. And my fantastic street team members who help share my books with every share, comment, and like!

And of course a big thank you to all of you, my readers! Without you I wouldn't be living my dreams of sharing the stories in my head with the world!

CHAPTER
One

July 30th
6:43 P.M.

Something was wrong.

Renee Miller's gut was all but screaming at her as she parked her car in the driveway of the house she shared with her long-term boyfriend.

Carefully, she scanned the yard and front of the house. The garden was just grass and two large oak trees, one on either side of the bricked path that ran from a gate in the white picket fence to the porch steps. Although she loved gardening, they kept the yard as simple as possible because Will was a former SEAL turned undercover cop and was often away for weeks or even months at a time. Between her job and caring for the house and yard alone, Renee had a vegetable garden and two flower beds, surrounded by a neat line of rocks in the backyard as that was about all she could manage in her busy schedule.

The simple garden meant there weren't many places that someone could hide and she couldn't see anyone hiding behind either of the thick tree trunks that provided shade on hot summer afternoons. Nor did she see anyone on the porch. The porch had been the deciding factor when they'd been looking at houses to buy. The prospect of lazy summer evenings sitting on the porch swing, side by side, sipping glasses of homemade lemonade was a picture that both she and Will had fallen in love with.

There were no cars parked out the front of the house, and she didn't see any figures, moving or otherwise at the corners of the house. There were no lights on, and nothing appeared to be hiding in any of the windows facing the street.

With no evidence to back up her gut feeling that something wasn't right, Renee climbed slowly from the car, collected her purse, laptop, and the stack of files she'd be reading through tonight, and closed and locked the car. Still cautious, she crossed to the porch steps and walked up them, half expecting someone to come jumping out at her at any second.

No one did, and slowly her uneasiness diminished.

Balancing her papers in her arms, she unlocked the door and stepped inside the quiet house, pausing to listen carefully for any signs that she wasn't alone before she closed the front door behind her.

She and Will had scrounged every dollar they could to afford this place, it was in a nice area, with good schools and lots of other families, which was important given that they both wanted children. The house was big enough for them to grow into, but not so big that it felt empty when it was just the two of them. At the moment, she stood in the house's more formal living area. There was a fireplace at one end with a lounge suite arranged around it, the other end had a large dining table, big enough to seat both her immediate family and his with one place to spare. In between the two areas was the grand piano, Will's pride and joy. You would never pick her huge, former SEAL, undercover cop, muscle mountain of a boyfriend as a classical pianist but Will was extremely talented.

The room was unoccupied, save for herself, and as she walked through to the back part of the house where they spent most of their time, Renee was starting to feel a bit silly. There was no one here, and her sudden case of nerves was probably due to the fact that Will had finished up a job yesterday and after not seeing him in almost three months, he would be coming home as soon as he finished up with all the paperwork his job entailed.

She couldn't wait to see him. Being with a SEAL had been hard, he'd been away so much, and when she did see him, he could never tell her anything about where he'd been and what he'd been doing. When he retired, she'd been excited to think that things would be different. Then he'd informed her that not only was he becoming a cop—something she had been anticipating knowing he couldn't turn off that protective side of himself—but he'd be working undercover. She didn't see him much, but she loved him and knew how important his job was, and she knew without a shadow of a doubt that Will loved her too, so somehow they found a way to make it work.

Convinced now that she was indeed alone, Renee dumped her armload of things on the kitchen table and hurried upstairs to change. She had graduated from law school three years ago and been working as a defense lawyer ever since. She worked for a firm that specialized in helping people who had been wrongly accused, and she was proud of the fact that she had already gotten a dozen wrongfully convicted men and women out of prison and returned to their lives.

Upstairs were three bedrooms, two shared a Jack and Jill bathroom, and the master had its own ensuite. Heading straight for her and Will's room, her gaze lingered on the bed for a moment, feeling her body heat as she thought of the hours she and Will would spend there when he got home, making up for the months they'd been apart.

Slipping on a pair of yoga pants and one of Will's old t-shirts that was more like a dress on her, but smelled of him and was one she often wore because it made her feel a teensy bit closer to him, she set the red dress she'd worn to work into the clothes hamper. Backtracking downstairs, she pulled a bottle of sparkling water from the fridge then decided she'd work for a while before eating just in case Will came home tonight and the two of them could share a meal. She took her bottle with her to the table and noticed she was missing a file. Assuming she'd dropped it in the other room, she went back into the front part of the house and immediately saw the missing file. She had indeed dropped it, and it lay just by the front door.

Renee hurried over to pick it up, but as she straightened, she froze.

The chain was on the front door.

She hadn't put it on when she came in.

Just as she was spinning around something slammed into her from behind.

She was shoved up against the wooden door, her head smashed into it so hard she saw stars.

A hand curled tightly into her long, dark hair, making tears prick her eyes at the stinging in her scalp, and she automatically raised her hands to try to ease the pressure.

"Don't do anything stupid," a low voice growled.

"P-please," she begged, "please don't do this. Let me go, please."

The man didn't say anything, just began to drag her through the house, away from the door and any hopes of escape she might have had. She struggled against him, her fingers clawing at the hand that held her, her body thrashing, her legs kicking, but it didn't do any good.

In the end, it didn't matter how hard she had trained in self-defense or that she was a near-perfect shot and had a gun upstairs in a lockbox in the back of the closet, this man was bigger and stronger than she was and that meant he could do what he wanted to her.

He pulled her into the kitchen, and she wondered briefly if he would take one of the knives from the block sitting neatly in a corner of the counter and slice her to shreds with it, but he kept going.

Toward the stairs.

And then she knew.

He was here to rape her.

"Let me go," she shrieked, renewing her efforts to break free. If she could just get out of his grip, she was sure she could make it to the back door, then once she was outside she could get to the street, and in this busy neighborhood there was always someone about.

A hand clamped over her mouth, and the pressure in her scalp disappeared as he wrapped one of his tree trunk-like arms across her chest. "I said don't be stupid," he growled in her ear.

This couldn't be happening.

It couldn't.

It had to be some sort of horrible nightmare.

Any second now she would wake up alone in her bed, or if she was lucky cocooned in the arms of the man she loved, and none of this would be real.

They were in her bedroom now, and he removed the hand from her mouth to roughly tie something over her eyes, plunging her into blackness.

And that was when she lost it.

She'd always had a fear of the dark, ever since as a kid, she'd been lost one summer in the forests surrounding the small town in which she had grown up. She'd been out there, alone, all night, before being found the following morning, and ever since the dark threw her back to that night.

Completely losing control, Renee screamed. She fought with everything she had, not really knowing what she was doing just knowing that she wasn't going down without having done everything within her power to survive.

She knew she connected with her attacker at least once because she heard his grunt of pain followed by a string of curses before she was thrown—literally picked up and thrown—across the room and into a wall.

The blow temporarily stunned her as pain bloomed from shoulder to hip down her left side.

Her attacker took advantage of that by picking her up and tossing her onto the bed like she weighed nothing, then proceeding to strip her clothes off and restrain and gag her.

It was over.

He had her right where he wanted her, naked and tied spread-eagled to her bed, a place that was supposed to be safe, a place where she spent her most intimate moments with the man she loved, a place that he was now going to desecrate.

Fear and panic unlike anything else she had ever experienced flooded through her system, tears streamed down her face, she choked on a sob that couldn't escape through the gag, her entire body shook so badly it hurt.

When the mattress dipped as he settled his weight between her legs, Renee prayed he killed her when he was done because she wasn't sure she could survive this.

~

7:50 P.M.

All he wanted was to get home, drag his girlfriend into his arms, kiss her, make love to her, and fall into a deep sleep with her snuggled close against his chest.

It had been a long eleven weeks since Will Black had seen his Renee and it was starting to get old. He and Renee had been together since they were in high school, he was two years older than she was and they'd started dating in his senior year. She had stood by him while he'd gone off to be a SEAL, waiting patiently for time together that was often few and far between. When he'd retired, Will knew that Renee had hoped that he would be coming home to her, but instead he'd become an undercover cop, asking her to once again sacrifice for his dreams.

Now he was wondering if it was time to give it up.

Not being a cop, he loved that and needed something to do where he could feed his adrenalin addiction and save innocent lives, but he was ready to give up undercover work. He wanted to be home more, spend more time with his girlfriend, with who he was ready to take the next step.

He and Renee loved each other and had he not spent the last decade away from more than he was home, he would have already asked her to marry him.

Finally, the timing was right.

He was twenty-eight now, he was ready for more out of life, he *wanted* more out of life. He wanted to make Renee his wife, he wanted kids and a dog. He wanted to go to sleep every night with her beside him and start each day with his lips on hers.

A smile tugged at his tired face as he drove toward home. Tonight was the night, he had the ring tucked safely in his pocket, and a dozen long-stemmed white roses because white was Renee's favorite color. He hadn't told her he was coming because he wanted to surprise her. As soon as he got inside he would get down on one knee, propose, then whisk her out for a fancy dinner, then when they returned home they'd make love like he had dreamed about every night over the last eleven weeks.

Eleven weeks was a long time, and it had made him realize that he couldn't be away from her for that long again.

Picturing the joy and delight that would light up Renee's pretty face when she saw him actually made him tear up. Him. The tough-as-nails SEAL turned undercover cop, the guy that prided himself on being in control of his actions twenty-four seven, no matter where he was or what he was doing.

Renee was his one weakness.

His kryptonite.

She was the light of his life, and he prayed that she knew it.

Renee had sacrificed so much more than he had in their relationship, now he wanted to be there to support her. He wanted her to know how much she meant to him, he wanted her to know that there wasn't anything he wouldn't do for her. He'd search the ends of the earth for her, he'd lay down his life for her, she was more precious to him than air, and it was time he told her.

Excitement washed away the exhaustion that came from almost three months of having to watch himself carefully so he didn't blow his cover and get himself killed. It wasn't just that he wanted to get enough evidence to close his case, it was that he had a reason to come home, and that meant he had to be as safe as he could be.

Turning into the street where the home he and Renee shared was, he couldn't help but imagine what their future held. There were families out for walks, kids sitting on dads' shoulders, dogs bouncing and straining against their leads, there were families playing in front yards, and kids riding bikes up and down the sidewalk. One day it would be him and Renee and their children enjoying summer evenings like this. He couldn't wait to be a dad, and he knew that Renee would be an amazing mom. In an ideal world, he'd love to have both a boy and a girl. He had one brother, and he'd been close with his cousins growing up. Three of them were boys with the baby of the family, Dahlia, the only girl.

Pausing to wait for a little boy of about four or five, who was learning to ride his bike without training wheels, and the kid's father to pass, he pulled his SUV into the driveway. Renee's car was there too since the garage was currently filled with planks of wood and tools for the gazebo he'd been planning on building in the backyard before he'd gone undercover this last time. He'd have to get on that, if he really was giving up undercover work then he'd have a lot more time to help Renee with the upkeep of their home.

As he turned the engine off, he got a feeling in his gut.

A feeling that said something was wrong.

Immediately, his hand went to his weapon. He'd spent enough years walking into dangerous, life-threatening situations to have learned to *always* believe what his gut was telling him. More times than he could count, it had saved his life, and the lives of his colleagues and this was even more important because this was his home and Renee was inside. If something was wrong it was her life on the line.

Scanning the yard, his eyes sought anything that was out of place but found nothing. Will knew that didn't mean anything and he carefully crossed the yard, blocking out the sounds of happy families, and checked the front door. It opened when he put his key in it but only a couple of inches, stopped by the chain.

Circling around the house, his gaze constantly moving, checking for anything that moved or anything that was out of place, he found the back door open.

Gun in hand, he entered his house, now knowing for certain that something was wrong. Renee's purse, laptop, and a stack of papers and files sat on the kitchen table, she was here, and while his protective instincts screamed at him to yell her name and go running wildly to find her, he somehow managed to cling to control.

Clearing the large, open space, he proceeded into the more formal front rooms, where he found a bottle of Renee's sparkling water on the floor by the door along with a file.

And blood.

There was blood on the door.

Will saw red.

Someone had hurt his woman.

Quickly, he cleared the rest of the downstairs before heading up the staircase. A bathroom joined two spare bedrooms that he checked all the while his brain was telling him to hurry up and get to the master suite.

At last he was standing outside the room he shared with the woman he loved, and even though his hand never shook on a mission it was shaking as he reached for the doorknob.

When the door swung open, he was met by his worst nightmare.

His beautiful, sweet, funny, caring, smart, wonderful girl lay naked on their bed, her hands and ankles tied to the bedposts, blindfolded and gagged.

Training fled his mind, and he ran to the bed, his fingers immediately reaching for his too-still girlfriend's neck. As soon as he touched her, Renee whimpered and tried to shrink away from him as much as her bonds allowed.

"It's okay, baby, it's me, it's Will," he soothed, pulling off the blindfold.

Terrified brown eyes found his, and he watched helplessly as they filled with tears. Knowing there was nothing he could say or do right now to make this better, he pulled out the small knife he kept on his keychain and cut the ropes binding her, removed the gag, then dragged her into his arms.

"Shh, sweetheart, I'm here, I've got you, baby," he crooned in Renee's ear as she sobbed.

There was blood on her head.

Bruises from shoulder to hip down her left side.

Blood and bruises on the inside of her thighs.

Someone had hurt the woman he loved.

Violated her.

Anger so strong it almost stole his breath coursed through his body so violently he was shaking with it.

When he found the man who had done this he would kill him.

Rip him to pieces with his bare hands.

That was a promise.

He wouldn't rest until Renee's attacker was dead.

For now though, he pulled a blanket free from the bed, tucked it around Renee and settled her on his lap, holding her tightly as he called for the cops and an ambulance.

"He'll pay, honey. The man who did this to you will pay," he promised as he pressed his lips to his shivering girlfriend's forehead, knowing that nothing short of death would prevent him from keeping that vow.

~

8:12 P.M.

She couldn't stop shaking.

Renee sat on Will's lap, burrowed as closely into his embrace as was possible. Tears streamed down her face, she couldn't stop them, couldn't even be bothered trying. What was the point? The man who broke in here had raped her, stolen something from her she could never get back. She would never be the same person ever again. Right now she wasn't even sure she had the strength to make it through this.

"Don't think that, honey," Will whispered, his lips against her forehead. "You are strong enough to get through anything. You hear me? *Anything.*"

Of course Will knew what she was thinking, he was Will. He knew everything about her, sometimes he even seemed to know more about her than she knew about herself. She loved him, and she knew he loved her too ... or at least he had.

How could he love her now?

He'd come home to find her tied up. It was pretty obvious what had happened to her. She was broken now, no longer whole, she felt ruined ... dirty. Would he still want to be with her knowing all of that? It wasn't like she would be able to hide it from him, he could practically see inside her soul.

"Sweetheart, it's going to be okay." If it was possible, he held her even tighter. "I love you, it's you and me together forever. We'll get through this together."

Why would he say that?

Why would he want to tie himself to someone broken like her?

What if she couldn't put herself back together?

There was no way she could ask him to walk this journey with her.

She should push him away, tell him to leave now, tell him that he deserved better than her, but she didn't. Instead, she grabbed fistfuls of his t-shirt, pressed her face against his chest, and another round of sobs flooded out.

"It's okay, shh, sweetheart, I'm here, I got you, you're okay," Will crooned in her ear, one arm holding her tight against him, while his other hand stroked her hair, her back, her face, anything he thought might soothe her.

But she was beyond soothing right now.

Renee had no idea how long she sat on Will's lap, crying and shaking, but suddenly the room was full of voices.

Was it him?

Had he come back?

Panic sliced through her, her heart tried to beat its way right out of her chest, and her breathing accelerated to the point where she was all but hyperventilating.

"Calm down, honey, it's okay, it's just the cops and paramedics," Will assured her. "The medics have a gurney, I'm just going to put you on it so they can check you out."

"No," she shrieked, clawing desperately at him. She needed him, he couldn't leave her. If he let her go she was sure she would fall apart.

"Okay, baby, okay, I won't let you go, I won't." His lips touched her forehead, her cheeks, the tip of her nose, feathering kisses designed to calm her, and it worked. Marginally. "I have to loosen my hold on you, just a little," he added quickly. "Just enough to let them check your pulse and blood pressure, maybe give you a little oxygen, and check on this bump on your head."

Because she knew there was no avoiding it, she didn't protest when Will loosened his grip on her, and a medic reached for her arm. Desperately, she tried to stamp down on the panic that tried to take hold of her. She was safe now, her assailant was gone and Will was here. He would never let anyone hurt her, as long as he was here by her side she was okay.

Until he left again.

She'd known he had finished his last assignment but how long until he went on another?

Sometimes she was lucky enough to have him all to herself for a couple of weeks before he left her again, but sometimes he was gone again within days. How long would it be this time? And how would she cope on her own?

"Honey, I'm going to pick you up now, okay? I'm going to carry you downstairs and out to the ambulance so we can get you to the hospital. I'm not going to leave you, I'll ride with you in the ambulance, and I'll be right by your side in the hospital," he promised.

Not sure she could speak without breaking into more tears, Renee just nodded and huddled closer when he stood with her in his arms and began to walk. Relief filled her when he stepped out of the bedroom. She never wanted to go in that room again or be in this house again. They'd have to sell it, buy a new place, one that wasn't tainted by violence.

The next hour or so passed in a blur. True to his word, Will held her in the ambulance, then held her hand while she was checked out in the ER, and was by her side as she endured the rape kit as best as she could.

By the time it was all done she was exhausted.

Although as exhausted as she was she didn't want to go to sleep. The idea of reliving what she'd just been through in her dreams was downright terrifying.

Just when she thought it was over for now and it would be just the two of them for a bit, the door opened, and a man and a woman walked into her hospital room. Thankfully, she'd been given a private room, she wasn't sure she could cope with strangers right now. Without being introduced she knew the newcomers were cops, which meant only one thing.

It was time to give her statement.

"Good evening, Ms. Miller," the woman said, giving her a sympathetic smile. "I'm Detective Astor, and this is Detective Phillips, and we need to ask you a few questions about what happened tonight."

Her scared eyes flew to Will's. Couldn't he make them go away? She wasn't sure she could handle this right now.

"It's okay, sweetheart, I know them both, and I'm not going

anywhere." He reached out and brushed a lock of hair off her cheek, tucking it behind her ear and letting his fingers caress her gently.

Renee nodded because there wasn't anything else she could really do right now. It was inevitable that she'd have to give her statement and maybe getting it over with now would be better, especially if Will was here. "It's Renee," she informed the detectives.

Detective Astor drew up a chair and sat close to the bed. "I know how hard this is, and we'll get it over with as quickly as we can. Why don't you start by walking us through what you remember and we'll go from there."

Dragging in a steadying breath, she tried to approach this from an as clinical and impersonal perspective as possible. "When I parked my car in the driveway I got this feeling that something wasn't right, but I couldn't see anyone in the yard or on the porch, so I thought I might be imagining it."

"Wait, you went inside the house even though your gut told you something was off?" Will demanded. His hazel eyes were hard, his reddish-brown hair a little longer than she was used to seeing on him, anger vibrated inside him, but she knew he was trying to stamp it down for her benefit.

"What else could I have done?"

"Not go inside," he said adamantly.

"I didn't know when you were coming home, and it's not like I could call the cops and say I had a bad feeling," she said reasonably. "I went inside, but there was no one there, and nothing looked touched so I convinced myself that it was nothing. I went upstairs and changed then came down intending to do a little work because I was hoping Will might be home to eat dinner with me later. There was a file missing, and I thought I might have dropped it so I went back to the front door and noticed the chain was on. I hadn't put it on, and that's when I knew ..." she broke off as she choked on a sob. None of this felt real, it was like a bad dream, she felt distanced from it all, but she knew that feeling wouldn't last forever. Sooner rather than later the full force of what had been done to her would sink in and she was terrified that when it did she would shatter.

"You're doing great," Detective Astor encouraged, and Will squeezed her hand supportively.

"Before I could turn around, someone grabbed me and shoved me into the wall. He grabbed my hair and began to pull me upstairs, I fought him, but it didn't do any good, he was too big. He got me upstairs, he threw me against the wall when I wouldn't stop fighting him, then he tied me to the bed, and he ..." she wasn't going to say the words, and she prayed they didn't force her to, right now it was just beyond her limits.

"Do you know who your attacker was?" Detective Astor asked.

"I never saw his face, and I didn't recognize his voice."

"Could it be someone related to your work? Someone after revenge?" Detective Phillips asked. He'd been hanging back, probably so as not to overwhelm her and in deference to the fact that she might be uncomfortable around strange men right now.

"I don't know, I guess it's possible," she shrugged. "The only part of him I saw was his arm. He was white, big muscles, and he had a tattoo."

Both Andrea and Phillip's eyes brightened at that piece of information. "Can you describe it to us?" Detective Astor asked.

Pleased to have something valuable to give the detectives and something to focus on that wasn't what she'd just lived through, Renee nodded vigorously. "I can do you one better. If you give me some paper and a pen, I can draw it for you."

~

8:12 P.M.

His woman was amazing.

Renee was in a hospital bed, had just been sexually assaulted, endured a rape kit, had a gash on her forehead and a lump the size of an egg, and yet here she was hunched over a table, a pen in her hand, carefully drawing a representation of the tattoo she had seen on her attacker.

If the tattoo was distinct enough to use it to ID the man who had assaulted her, the cops better hope they got to him before he did. These were his colleagues, he respected them, he liked them, he and Andrea had even gone undercover together before, but when it came to dealing with this situation it would be handled his way if he had any say in it. This man had hurt the woman he loved, violated her in the most horrendous way possible, and for that he had to die.

A long, slow, painful death.

Anger was a living thing inside him, Will was struggling to keep it under control, he wanted to hit something—no, strike that, he wanted to trash something, the hospital, his house, the entire world. He was doing his best to keep it under control because Renee needed him right now.

She *needed* him.

She needed him to do something, to somehow make this better for her.

He had to make this better.

Will knew he couldn't erase what had happened or the effects it would have on her life, although if it were possible he would do it in a heartbeat.

There was only one thing that he could give Renee that might marginally ease the turmoil she would have to battle through. He could give her closure. He could find the man who hurt her and make sure he was dead so that maybe she could find a way past the fear that he knew was soon to be a large part of her life.

While he struggled to stand still, keeping his place at Renee's bedside, a hand resting lightly between her shoulder blades, she worked diligently on her drawing. Renee had always been a talented artist, he knew that her forte was watercolor painting, but give her anything that could make a mark and she would create you a masterpiece.

This time was no different.

Neither of the detectives spoke, no one wanted to break the spell and ruin Renee's concentration, so they all just waited. Renee seemed to have blocked them all out, focused on her task, something that no doubt gave her a brief reprieve from thinking about her assault.

It killed him that she would never be the same woman again.

You couldn't live through what Renee had and not be changed.

How much she would change remained to be seen.

Will knew his woman, and he knew that she would fight her way through this. She would conquer her fears and rise from the ashes stronger than she had been before because that was just the kind of person that she was.

"Done," Renee announced triumphantly, holding up the sheet of paper with the drawing on it. She had drawn a devil's face on a hand connected to a snake's body that curled around the forearm disappearing up into the sleeve of a t-shirt.

As soon as he saw it his heart sank.

He knew that tattoo.

That would be a good thing if it belonged to one person, but the symbol that Renee had just drawn belonged to a motorcycle club. A notorious MC club that was well known for its use of drugs and women. Most club members sported the tattoo so there was no way to know which one of them had committed the crime, and there was no way that Andrea and Phillip could just go waltzing in there asking questions. No one in that club would turn on another. Which meant that while they knew where to look for the rapist they weren't going to be getting any answers.

Unless ...

"Why isn't anyone saying anything?" Renee asked. She turned her head to look up at him, her worried eyes seeking his, needing reassurance.

"Are you sure?" Detective Astor asked.

"Yes, this is the tattoo the man had," she replied confidently. "You know who this belongs to, don't you?"

He hated knowing who had hurt her, he hated that he had to tell her, and to be honest he had to wonder why her attacker had left her alive. Had the man fled the house when he'd arrived home? Had the attacker been watching Renee for a while, learning her routines, and believed she lived alone and he would have had more time to finish her off?

That sent a shiver slicing through him.

He could have lost her.

"Will?" Renee sounded more panicked, and he knew they had to tell her.

Sitting on the bed beside her, he wrapped an arm around her shoulders and drew her close. "The tattoo is a symbol for a motorcycle club, the Devil's Snakes, you've probably heard of them."

Her dark eyes grew wide and frightened. "Someone from an MC club attacked me? Why?"

"I don't know, baby. They're into drugs and women, but I doubt this was anything official unless you've dealt with anyone from the club in a case lately."

She shook her head.

"Then it's likely that the man who attacked you just happens to be in the club."

"But if a lot of members have this same tattoo then how will you find the one who hurt me?" she asked, bottom lip wobbling. She was struggling to hold it together now that she didn't have something else to focus on.

"I will find him, Renee, you have my word on that, I don't want you to worry about it." Leaning down, he kissed her forehead, then hesitated above her lips. After what she'd been through, did she want him to kiss her? He'd never before had to worry about whether the woman he loved wanted him to kiss her, but things had changed, and since he didn't know how much it left him uncertain. Deciding that if Renee didn't want his lips on hers she would have turned away, he brushed a light kiss across her mouth. "I need to talk to the detectives for a moment. Why don't you close your eyes, try to rest a little?"

"Are you leaving?" she asked, fear evident on her face and in her voice, and he hated that she was afraid to be alone.

"No, sweetheart, we'll be right outside your door."

"Okay," she agreed. As he released his hold on her she shrunk down into the bed, pulling the covers up to her chin, and curled into herself. She looked so small, so vulnerable, so fragile, and he had to remind himself that no one was tougher than Renee, she would get through this.

Outside Renee's room, he paced up and down, tearing his fingers through his hair. This was tearing him up inside but he didn't see any other option, there was no way he could allow the man who had hurt his Renee go unpunished.

But still ...

Leaving? Could he do that?

It he didn't then who else could?

He'd done a stint undercover with the Devil's Snakes, his cover should still be intact, and he was sure he could get his boss to sign off on it. As far as they were concerned he'd gone to prison, he could easily pretend he'd just gotten out and reassimilate in, tracking down the man who had assaulted Renee.

Still to do that he'd have to leave, and Renee needed him. His fingers tightened in his hair until he felt his scalp sting. This was the only way he could get Renee justice but that didn't mean it wouldn't kill him to not be by her side.

This wasn't how he had envisioned tonight turning out, he'd been ready to quit, but how could Renee ever get past this if the man who had hurt her wasn't found and punished?

If he could give her that then it would be worth it.

He hoped.

Will turned to the other two cops. "I'm going to go undercover in the Devil's Snakes, it's the only way to find which one of them did this."

Two shocked sets of eyes looked back at him. "You're going to go undercover? Are you sure that's what you want to be doing right now?" Detective Astor asked.

No, he wasn't sure, but it was the only he could do to make this better. "She needs to know she's safe. How else can she recover?" he demanded fiercely. It would gut him not to be by her side through these next few days or weeks, but how could Renee even begin to work through all of this with that man still out there? He had to do this for her it was that simple.

"Why don't you give us a chance to work this first," Detective Phillips suggested. "Then if things don't work out you can try going in."

"They won't talk to you, and we all know it. This is the only way, I wish it weren't, I wish there was something else we could do, but she needs this. She won't be alone, I'm going to call her parents and have them come and stay with her." This wasn't how he wanted this to go down, he wanted to be there to hold Renee when she had nightmares, to kiss away her tears, to assure her as many times as she needed to hear it that she could do this.

But that wasn't the way this would happen.

At least not just yet.

Over the next few minutes he made a phone call to his boss to get the okay to go undercover in the Devil's Snakes, then to Renee's family. By the time he was ready to go back into her room to break the news a nurse was walking toward him.

"I'm about to go in and give Ms. Miller something to help her sleep," the nurse told him.

"Can you hold off just a couple of minutes? There's something I need to tell her."

The nurse nodded but said firmly, "Five minutes."

As soon as he entered Renee's room, she lifted her head and smiled at him. "You're back."

"I am, but I have to tell you something," he said, sitting on the edge of the bed and taking her hands in his.

"Something's wrong," she said immediately.

"No, honey, not wrong, but," he dragged in a breath knowing it was better to just say it and get it out there, "I'm going to go undercover in the club to find out who hurt you."

Her brow creased. "When?"

"Now, tonight."

She bolted upright. "You're leaving now?" she asked shrilly.

"As soon as your parents get here, I won't leave until then."

"You're leaving," she said it like she couldn't believe it.

"I have to, sweetheart, I have to find the man who hurt you so that you can feel safe again."

"I'll never feel safe again," she countered, snatching her hands from his grip. "I need you, Will, don't leave me, please," she begged.

"I won't be gone long, I promise, I need to do this for you."

"But—" she was cut off when the nurse entered the room.

"I'm going to give you something to help you get some rest, Ms. Miller," the middle-aged woman announced, injecting something into Renee's IV.

"Please, Will," she begged again, "please be here when I wake up. Don't walk away, not now. I love you, I need you, don't go."

He took the hand she stretched toward him and helped her get settled against the pillows as the drug began to take effect. He pressed a kiss to her lips, then stroked her hair as she drifted off, but he didn't promise that he would be here when she woke up because he wouldn't be. He would give her the closure she needed by finding the man who hurt her and killing him.

CHAPTER
Two

Nine Months Later

April 24th
5:57 P.M.

Sinking onto the sofa, Renee groaned as her tired body tried to relax.

Relaxation was not something that had been a part of her life for the last ten months.

Ever since *that* night.

The night that changed not just herself, but her life as well.

Keeping busy was the only way she had survived. She had thrown herself into work, taking on a heavier caseload because that way she could think about other people's problems instead of her own. She had taken to working out, buying herself a treadmill and a weight set so she wouldn't have to leave her home, but could work off all her nervous energy. She kept the TV on at all times, playing something in the background she wasn't interested in, but the noise meant she didn't spend her time straining in the quiet to hear something. Her life wasn't what it had been, but she was coping the best way she knew how.

Alone.

Despite her begging him not to leave, Will had already been gone by the time she'd woken up in the hospital the morning after her assault.

She'd been shocked, hurt, betrayed, and angry. He had abandoned her when she needed him the most, deciding for himself what she needed rather than just asking her. Renee hadn't heard from him since, and she didn't expect to hear from him again. He'd made his choice, and it wasn't her.

Will might not have been there for her, but her family had been. Her parents had divorced when she was eight, and things had been rocky for a while. There'd been times where they fought over her and her siblings and times when neither parent seemed to want to be bothered with their children, but things had improved once she'd become an adult. Both her parents and all three of her siblings had been there when she opened her eyes. Her mother had even moved in with her for six months, and while it had been a terrifying step, eventually she'd known that she needed to rebuild her life and learn to be on her own again so she'd told her mom it was okay to leave.

Now it was just her.

She still had nightmares and flashbacks, she didn't trust anyone and limited the amount of time she was outside of her house; basically work was about it. She had her groceries delivered, and since she'd sold the house and moved into an apartment in a secure building that was monitored around the clock, she loved that the doormen collected her packages so she didn't have to see anyone she didn't know. As much as she hated it, strangers scared her. What if they wanted to hurt her? That fear was always at the back of her mind, and she hadn't learned to master it.

Yet.

But she would.

Renee was determined to get back to the woman she had been before. She attended weekly therapy sessions, and she'd taken medication for a while but weaned herself off them a couple of months ago. She faced her fears, and she conquered them one by one.

SOME TRUTH CAN BE DISTORTED

Each victory she achieved made her confidence grow. Maybe she really could do this.

Her stomach grumbled, and she debated getting up and making some dinner. It was only six, she had plenty of time, and while she was hungry she wasn't in the mood to eat just yet. Pushing herself off the soft pillows, she sat up and reached for her laptop. She'd work for a couple of hours, then eat, then a workout, shower, and off to bed.

Going to bed was still something she struggled with and frequently avoided, sleeping on the couch instead. She'd sold the bed that used to be hers and Will's, it brought back too many bad memories. Not just of her assault, but of the nights she'd spent there with Will.

Will Black.

He'd broken her heart when he'd left.

It felt like their entire life together had been a lie.

He wasn't the man she thought he was.

She had believed that he loved her, that he would do anything for her, but instead, he'd made a selfish decision, he'd gone after her attacker because it was what *he* wanted, not because it was what *she* needed.

Dwelling on this wasn't productive. It was what it was, there was no going back. Even if Will turned up on her doorstep right now she wouldn't take him back. She couldn't.

Her stomach grumbled again, and she realized it wasn't going to be silent and let her work so she may as well eat first. Renee no longer ate for pleasure, her body needed fuel so she ate, it was as simple as that.

She stood, stretched, and had taken three steps toward the kitchen when there was a knock on her door.

She froze.

Who was it?

Her parents and siblings knew better than to show up unannounced and scare her so it wasn't them. The doormen always called up to tell her if there was a parcel or something she needed to attend to, they wouldn't just come up to the twelfth floor and knock on her door. A neighbor maybe? While she couldn't be described as sociable anymore, she occasionally spoke with some of the other people who lived on her floor so it was a possibility that it was one of them.

With hands that shook more than she would have liked, she walked over to the door and activated the screen on the wall beside it that would show her who was out there.

She gasped when she saw who it was.

Her knees wobbled, and she quickly leaned against the wall to remain upright.

It couldn't be.

It wasn't possible.

There was another knock, but she couldn't move right now, she could barely breathe. How could this be happening?

"Renee? I know you're in there, can you let me in, please?"

She didn't want to. She wanted to pretend that this wasn't happening, that he had stayed gone, she wasn't sure she could handle this.

"Please, sweetheart."

The plea stabbed her in the heart, and even though she knew this was a bad idea, she somehow managed to unlock and open the door leaving her standing face to face with Will.

Part of her wanted to throw herself into his arms, hold onto him, soak in his strength, let him comfort her and take care of her, but the rational side of her brain reminded her that he had left her and that she had managed on her own, she didn't need someone to look after her. So she stood her ground and just looked at him. He looked exhausted. There were dark marks under his red eyes, there were lines in his face that hadn't been there before, and his entire demeanor was defeated.

Anger rushed through her.

Why was he the one looking like he'd been hurt?

He was the one who had left her even though she'd begged him not to.

Planting her hands on her hips, she frowned at him. "How did you get up here? The doormen know not to let anyone up without telling me."

"I showed them my badge, told them it was official police business."

That he'd tricked his way up here only added fuel to her anger. He'd probably implied she was a suspect in something, now the doormen wouldn't be so disposed to help her out, and she'd have to face more strangers on her own than she was comfortable with.

If he was here, then she knew what that meant.

Her attacker was either dead or in prison.

Despite her anger, relief flooded through her. It was nice to know she didn't have to worry about him coming back.

Will took a tentative step inside her apartment. "He's in prison, he won't ever hurt you again."

"I suspected that if you're here." Although part of her had thought Will wouldn't be able to let the man live.

"How are you?" His voice was tortured, and his hands were curled into fists as though it were the only way he could stop himself from touching her.

Renee was infinitely glad for his restraint because if he touched her, she was sure she would melt at his feet. She might be angry with him, but she still loved him. Unfortunately, he had proven that love wasn't enough. So many times over the course of their relationship she had wondered if deep down Will loved his job more than her. It wasn't that she thought he didn't love her, she knew that he did, but they had been together for a decade and he hadn't proposed. He had gone from one job where he was away for months at a time to another, and then when she had needed him the most he hadn't been there for her.

"If you'd wanted to know how I was doing you could have been there," she reminded him, but without malice as her anger drained away. She couldn't be angry with him for doing the same thing he'd always done, especially when she had always given him the impression it was okay to put his job before her, but she was hurt, and she knew that she had to be strong, taking him back wasn't an option.

"I wanted to give you closure," he implored, begging her with his eyes to believe him.

"You wanted to get yourself revenge," she corrected. "I needed you, I asked you to stay, and you chose not to. It was over between us the second you walked out that hospital door leaving me behind."

"Don't say that, please, Renee." He reached out a hand, but she took a step back, she knew her limits, and she would cave in a second if he touched her.

"It is what it is, Will. Please don't make this any harder than it has to be. You broke my heart when you left, and there's no going back. Thank you for letting me know that he's in prison now. Goodbye," she said as she reached for the door, making it clear in as nice a way as she could that he wasn't welcome here.

"Can we just talk for a bit, please?"

"No," she said firmly. She'd fought so hard to get strong again, and she wasn't going to let someone back into her life who had proven to her that she couldn't trust him. "I need you to leave, Will. I don't want to fight, I need you to go."

"I love you." Tears shimmered in his hazel eyes, it was the first time she had ever seen him this close to crying, and it almost weakened her resolve.

"I love you too, but that isn't what this was about. I don't trust you anymore. Instead of putting my needs first, you put your own, at a time when I was vulnerable I couldn't count on you. It's over, Will. There's no going back, what we had is gone. Sometimes love isn't enough."

He opened his mouth, then closed it again. Reached out a hand but let it fall away. Then his head dropped, and without another word, he turned and walked out of her apartment.

Walked out of her life.

That was it.

It was done.

Over.

She'd known it, but now it felt so final.

This wasn't what she wanted, but she knew it was what was best for her. How could she build a life with someone who had shown her that when she was at her lowest he wouldn't be there to lift her up? Once trust had been broken, shattered, sometimes it just couldn't be put back together.

Renee closed the door, locked it, then leaned her back against it and sunk until her bottom hit the floorboards. She brought her knees up to her chest and wrapped her arms around herself, tucking her chin in.

"Goodbye, Will," she whispered as the tears came.

She didn't know what the future held for her, she didn't know if anyone but Will would ever own her heart, but she knew that she was strong enough to get through this, to keep going. She'd gotten this far on her own, and maybe one day her life would change from just surviving to actually living.

CHAPTER
Three

April 25th
3:06 A.M.

He'd had it all, and he'd lost it.

No.

Not lost it, he'd thrown it away.

Will hadn't realized until the moment he saw her that it had been a mistake to go undercover to catch the man who assaulted her. Up until that second, he had believed that he was doing the right thing, doing what she needed him to do, but now he wasn't so sure.

Everything was so messed up.

It felt like things had spun out of control so quickly, he knew it had been ten months, but it felt like just yesterday he'd arrived home to find Renee tied to their bed. That night had changed everything, he'd been so happy, planning to propose, planning on changing his job so he could be around for her more often, now he'd lost her. When he'd made the decision to go undercover he'd thought he'd be gone a couple of weeks, maybe a month or two tops, not ten.

Now it was too late. He'd ruined what they'd had, lost the best thing that had ever happened to him, and what was worse was that he'd hurt her. He hadn't been there when she needed him, he hadn't been there to brush away her tears or keep her nightmares at bay. He hadn't been there for her, and that made him feel like his heart had been ripped out of his body.

His beautiful, sweet, angel and he'd hurt her.

"Hey, man."

Will started at the sound and looked up to find his cousin Abe standing over him. Abe was the oldest of the Black kids, older than him by eleven and a half months. Growing up, he had been just as close to Abe, and Abe's brothers Levi and Theo, as he had been to his brother Julian. Both he and Abe had inherited their Irish fathers' reddish-brown hair, as had the littlest Black, Abe's baby sister, Dahlia.

Maybe he should be surprised that his cousin had known where to come looking for him, but he wasn't. When he'd found the man he was looking for and his undercover assignment was over, he'd gone home only to find that Renee had sold up and moved. They'd put only her name on the house, since he was undercover most of the time it had just seemed like the sensible thing to do, so she'd been able to sell it while he'd been away. Sweet thing that she was, she'd given his half of the money to his father, it had been waiting for him when he came back. When he had called her father to ask if he knew where Renee was, he was sure his father had spread the word around the family that he was back and things weren't going to go well when he spoke with Renee.

"Not now, okay, Abe," he said, returning his gaze to the river before him. He'd come out to a place that he had loved as a kid, a place where he and his brother, their cousins, dad, and uncle had spent many a summer camping and fishing. When he got older, he'd brought Renee out here as well. This was the spot where they had made love for the first time. They'd both been virgins, he'd been seventeen and about to start his senior year, and Renee had been fifteen, nearly a sophomore. They'd already been dating for almost two years, but he'd wanted to wait until Renee was ready.

He remembered that night like it was yesterday.

It was a warm summer evening, he'd made them a fire, more for atmosphere than warmth. He'd caught fish for dinner and cooked it for her over the flames, he'd picked her flowers, and they'd lain on their backs, looking up at the stars and talking for hours. Then she'd taken his hand, led him into the tent, and they'd spent the night making love. It had been a little awkward their first time, but by the time the sun rose they'd learned so much about each other's bodies.

"You're still here," he said when he realized Abe was still standing beside him.

"I don't think you should be alone tonight."

"I'm not really in the mood to talk," he said, resting back against the wooden bench he and his brother and cousins had carved from a fallen tree one summer when they were in their early teens.

His cousin didn't say anything, just walked around him and sat at the other end of the bench, tipping his head up and looking at the stars.

They sat in silence for a while, Will lost in thought, trying to understand how he had made such a horrible mistake. Was Renee right? Had he been selfish? Had he put his needs before hers? He had been so positive that he was giving her what she needed, but it was obvious he'd been wrong.

"I messed up," he said at last.

"Yeah, you did," Abe returned.

"Hey." He swung a half-hearted fist at his cousin's shoulder. "Aren't you supposed to be here to give me a pep talk, tell me everything will work out, that it will all be okay in the end?"

"I never said that was why I was here," Abe replied calmly. His cousin was well known for his calm, unflappable nature. It had made him a fabulous SEAL, and made him a great sheriff. It also made him a frustrating friend. He wanted to hear that he'd done the right thing, that he still had a chance at winning Renee back, that he hadn't screwed everything up so badly it was unfixable.

"Then why are you here?"

"To make sure you don't do anything stupid."

"It's a little late for that." If he could just rewind the clock ten months there were so many things he would do differently. Starting with getting home earlier that night so that Renee never got hurt. But if he had been too late to prevent her getting hurt then he would have done as she'd asked and stayed by her side, he wouldn't have left her to deal with everything alone.

"Are you sure?"

"Renee told me it was over. She seemed pretty clear, she was angry at first, but then she was just sad." He would have preferred Renee to scream and yell and vent rather than standing there with tears shimmering in her pretty dark eyes. "She said she still loves me, but she doesn't trust me, and I don't know how to fix that."

"So you're giving up?"

"I don't know what else to do. She asked me not to make things harder for her. How can I fight for her knowing that it's going to cause her more pain? She deserves to be free, she deserves happiness. She deserves everything I can't give her."

"So what are you going to do? Go back to working undercover?"

"No, I had already decided to give it up before this happened."

"If you're looking for a fresh start, why don't you stay in River's End, work for me? Richard Long just retired, and I've been looking for a new deputy. I'd love to have you working with me and Julian, and you'd be closer to family again. It's up to you, but I think it makes sense."

Right now that was as good a plan as any. He couldn't stay near Renee because he wasn't sure he could honor her wishes and stay away, nor was he convinced that he should. Maybe this was a good distraction. Starting over here would help take his mind off the mistakes he'd made and the mess he'd made of his relationship with Renee.

"You serious?" he asked.

"Completely."

"Then I accept."

"Happy to have you onboard." Abe slapped his shoulder and then stood. "Come on, let's get out of here. Are you staying with your dad or do you want to bunk with me for a bit?"

To be honest, he hadn't thought that far ahead. He'd just gotten into his car after seeing Renee and ended up here. "I'll stay with you, shouldn't take me long to find a place. I'll meet you there, I just need to do something first."

Abe nodded and then hiked off through the forest. Will stood and walked closer to the water. It was a clear night and moonlight sparkled on the dark water, it was beautiful here.

Reaching into his pocket, he pulled out the small velvet box and opened it, staring at the ring inside. In his mind, he could picture what it would look like on Renee's delicate finger, but it didn't look like that was meant to be.

Snapping the box closed, he lifted it, intending to toss it into the river, but he couldn't. He couldn't let go. There had to be hope for them, however slim that one day they would find their way back to one another. They still loved each other, and that had to count for something.

Slipping the box back into his pocket, he turned and headed for his car. He didn't know what the future held, but he knew one thing, Renee would always be the love of his life and the owner of his heart.

CHAPTER
Four

Sixteen Months Later

August 2nd
9:14 A.M.

Back in River's End.

As soon as she made the turn into the road that would lead her to Main Street, it was like she had never left.

Not that it was necessarily a bad thing.

Renee needed a break from her life.

She had made a mess of things, a mess she didn't know how to handle, and she was embarrassed to say that her return here was her running away. Of course she wasn't proud to admit that, but it was what it was, and after everything she had faced over the last two years maybe she was entitled to take a timeout from life.

With a weary sigh, she scrubbed a hand down her face as she drove through River's End's main shopping area. This place was a sweet, quaint little town, and the shopping area was adorable. It was summer, and there were plenty of tourists, people out camping in the forest and up the mountain that the town was nestled at the base of. There were people here to enjoy the river and the many recreational activities it afforded.

People bustled about, laughing and talking, and she couldn't help but envy them. Had she ever been like that?

Of course Renee knew that she had been, she'd been carefree, happy, enjoying life, but that seemed so long ago now that she could hardly even remember what that had been like. Everything had changed that night a little over two years ago, she had changed, and although she had fought hard, she still wasn't the same person she'd been before.

It was like that spark, that essence that everyone had that transformed them from merely a living organism to a human being, had been stolen from her and she didn't know how to get it back. The nightmares had faded over time, as had the flashbacks, she had found a way to forge forward, but she couldn't remember the last time she had laughed—or even smiled—and it wasn't faked to make people think she was normal.

Since she mostly kept to herself—keeping things distant with her colleagues, staying away from her family as much as possible, limiting time with friends, and avoiding anything that even smelled of a relationship—it wasn't so hard to do.

Still, she had plenty of new issues to worry about without dredging up the traumas of her past.

Navigating through the town, she turned into her mother's driveway and parked her car. It was weird to be back here, she hadn't been to her mother's house in probably close to five years now. This was the house she had grown up in, the house where she and her siblings had huddled together in one of their bedrooms during one of their parents' heated arguments. After the divorce, they had bounced between this place and their father's new house. Splitting their time between two homes had been hard but at least she'd had her brother and sisters.

The front door opened and her mother came barreling down the path in her energetic way. Her mother always reminded her of a bumblebee, bright, always buzzing about, sweet but watch out for her stinger because if you did something she didn't like you could expect to be stung.

"Renee, darling, I'm so excited to see you," Kim Turner sang as she flung her arms around Renee as soon as she stepped out of the car.

"Hi, Mom." Her mother was hard to spend time around because she was so self-involved and so high maintenance that it was exhausting. Still, she'd been a lifesaver two years ago when she'd given up everything to stay with her for six months as she recovered from the psychological injuries her assault had inflicted. All in all her mom meant well, she was just draining to spend time with.

"Thank you so much for housesitting for us, darling," her mom continued as she waved a hand at her newest boyfriend who was standing on the doorstep. Since the divorce was final her mother had rarely gone more than a month or two without a man, but she'd never gotten past the girlfriend stage, whether it was because she just hadn't found the one or she was gun shy about getting married again Renee wasn't sure.

"It's no problem," she assured her mother as she opened her little car's trunk and removed her suitcase. "I needed a break and to just get away from everything for a while, hanging out here, going for walks in the forest, and swims in the river. It's just what I need."

"I'm so glad we both get to help each other out then," her mom gushed. "Ben, come help Renee with the suitcase," she called out to her boyfriend.

Ben obediently came trotting over and took the suitcase from her hand, giving her a kiss on the cheek. "Nice to see you again, Renee."

She met Ben—boyfriend number fourteen in the last twenty years —maybe twice in the four months since they'd been together, but he seemed like a nice enough guy and her mom seemed to like him. Renee lived about three hours away, and since she was usually busy with her job, her mom would drive up about once a month, and the two of them would have lunch or catch a movie, maybe have their nails done. She enjoyed those days but was always glad to see her go so she could return to her quiet, little life.

"Nice to see you too, Ben. Bet you're looking forward to the cruise."

"Can't wait." He grinned as the three of them headed for the front door.

"Speaking of which, we'd better get going, dear. I want to do a little last-minute shopping when we get there," her mom said.

"What time is your flight?" she asked as they stepped inside out of the heat.

"In about two hours."

"Then you're cutting it close." The airport was about thirty minutes away, and although they weren't taking an international flight, they still had to get through security.

"You're right, we'd better hustle. Ben, be a dear and take the suitcases out to the cab, it's just pulled up." When Ben went to do that she turned to Renee. "There are leftovers in the fridge that should hold you over a day or two, the cats have been fed and shouldn't be any bother, and you can stay in your old room."

"Okay, thanks for leaving some stuff for me," she said, grateful her mother had known that a trip to the store wouldn't be something she'd be up to the first day she was back here. She was staying for two months so she knew she couldn't hide out here indefinitely and that already her presence back in town was probably circulating the local gossip route, but at least she didn't have to face anyone today.

"Of course, sweetheart. Call if you need anything, and I'll let you know when we land and when we board the ship."

"Have fun."

"We will I'm sure."

They exchanged hugs and kisses, then Renee stood in the doorway and waved as her mom and Ben got in the car and drove off down the street. When the car was out of sight she closed the door, then leaned against it and sighed.

It was weird being back.

As much as she loved the town she had grown up in, she knew that as soon as she left the house and people knew she was back she would be inundated with questions. That everyone in town knew what had happened to her was a given, she wasn't even going to pretend to hope that was a secret, they would know, and being the gossip-hungry place that any small town was they were going to bring it up. Not outright, they wouldn't come straight out and mention her rape, but they would hint around it, wanting to know how she was doing and what had happened between her and Will Black.

Will.

There wasn't a day that had gone by in the last sixteen months that she hadn't thought about him. She knew she'd made the right choice— really the only choice she could have given the situation—but that didn't mean her heart didn't ache every time she thought of him.

He was not only her first love but her only love, and she'd been so sure they were going to spend forever together.

You'd think two years would have been enough for her to accept that wasn't happening, but it was hard because she had wanted it so badly it often brought her to tears, but she knew she couldn't have it.

Pushing off the door, she headed into the kitchen to make herself some breakfast, at least being back in River's End would solve one of her problems. Between worrying over Will and what had happened to tear them apart, and the questions she knew were coming, she was going to have hardly any time to worry about the mess she'd left behind when she'd fled back to her old home.

～

10:24 A.M.

"Long night?"

Will looked over at his cousin, standing lounging against the wall beside the table in the Sheriff's offices where they kept the coffee and an array of homemade baked goods. "Yeah, long night," he agreed. He paused and gave Abe an assessing once over. His cousin had a smile on his face, his eyes were bright and sparkling, and his posture was relaxed. After six months of seeing the transformation in Abe it still shocked him sometimes. It was like his cousin had become a whole new person ever since he met the love of his life.

"What?" Abe asked, straightening and picking up another donut.

"You look good is all, relaxed."

"You'd look good too if you slept through the night for the first time in two months," Abe replied with a grin.

"Baby girl made it all night without a feed, huh?" he asked, walking over and pouring himself a badly needed cup of caffeine. Will knew his cousin hadn't meant anything by the comment, but it had been a *long* time since he had slept through the night. Not since the last night he had spent with Renee in his arms well over two years ago.

Quickly, he shut down that train of thought because thinking of Renee was opening a can of worms better left closed.

"Yeah, the little princess slept all night, and it was wonderful." Abe beamed that special smile that always lit his face whenever they talked about his two-month-old daughter.

"You're one lucky guy. That baby is just the sweetest thing ever." He smiled and hoped it reached his eyes. It wasn't that he was jealous, or not really anyway. He knew that Abe had gone through a lot and he was glad that his cousin had found someone who loved him. Abe was living a dream he hadn't even known he wanted until Meadow Smith came into his life, and now they and their baby daughter were living their happy ever after.

If he and Renee were still together, they'd be married by now, maybe even have a baby of their own.

You'd think that sixteen months would be long enough for thoughts of her and their life together and the future they could have shared to have faded, but Will missed her as much today as he did that night nearly a year and a half ago where she had ended things.

Abe didn't seem to notice his melancholy. "Dawn is the best baby ever, she's so placid, and she hardly ever cries, and that smile of hers, I don't know how I'm going to say no to her when she gets older."

"She's going to be one spoiled little princess," he agreed. The whole family was in love with that baby. His aunt and uncle were the proudest grandparents he'd seen, Abe's brothers Levi, and his girlfriend Sydney, and Theo, and his pregnant fiancée Maggie, all doted on the little girl, as did he, his brother Julian, and their father.

"Meadow is going to have to be the one to discipline her," Abe said with a chuckle. "Imagine that, the retired SEAL turned sheriff can't even discipline his own daughter."

"I think Meadow can handle it," he teased. He might regret how things had ended with Renee, but he didn't resent Abe, or Levi, and Theo, finding their other half.

"Meadow can handle anything," Abe agreed, beaming with pride. "She's an amazing mother already, the way she handles midnight feeds, and diapers, and exhaustion, and still tends to the house and cooks and goes to work, she's phenomenal. Some days I just stand and stare at her in awe."

"Yeah, man, that's awesome," he said, quickly turning away as his throat threatened to close up and choke him. He'd had that, he'd had a phenomenal woman and he'd let her get away. He was a fool. "I'm going to fill in some paperwork then head home for a couple of hours sleep."

Before he could escape to his desk, Abe asked, "Everything okay?"

"Fine," he replied tightly. A discussion about Renee was the last thing he wanted right now. Since he couldn't have her in his life again, he just wanted to forget about her, move on. No, that wasn't true, what he wanted was to go to her, make her listen to him, and beg her to take him back, apologize as many times as it took to make it happen.

"We still having trouble with Raphael?" Abe asked, apparently assuming his mood was because of working all night and not because of all their talk of happy marriages and adorable babies with big smiles.

For a small town, River's End had had more than its fair share of violence these last few months. From Meadow's ex following her here and leaving a trail of bodies in his wake, to Maggie Wilson being targeted, and then the murders last spring, Will really didn't want this to become anything.

"I wish I could say we weren't, but we are," Will reluctantly replied. "Things are getting worse, not better, and his drinking is getting out of control."

Raphael Russo had moved to River's End around the time he'd left for BUD/S training to become a SEAL. He'd gotten involved with the daughter of the pastor at the town's church, and things had started going downhill from there. He'd gotten Mary pregnant when they were both just nineteen, then split, leaving her alone to give birth to and raise their baby. When he'd returned, he'd all but been run right back out of town for having disgraced the minister's family.

Apparently, Raphael and Mary hadn't been done with each other because she'd turned up pregnant again, Raphael was the father, and the two had seemed to be making a go of it for a while. Raphael did some handyman jobs around town, but when it became clear he was drinking on the job after several accidents, he was run out of town again.

Like an addiction neither of them could break, Raphael and Mary kept getting drawn to one another. Another baby later and the stress of no money and three little mouths to feed became too much, and Raphael started taking his drunken anger out on Mary. Over the last decade or so the man had been in and out of prison. Whenever he was home he and Mary seemed to make another baby, they now had seven to care for and no real income to make it happen. It was to the point where it seemed like every other night either Will or one of the other deputies was over at the small, rundown farm dragging a drunken Raphael away from his woman or one of his kids.

"I don't know what to do about him, Abe, something has to break but I don't see what. The guy is in and out of prison so much he may as well get his mail sent there, and it doesn't seem to have any effect on his drinking or his aggression." If there was one thing Will couldn't stand it was a guy who beat up on his woman and his kids, he didn't get why Mary didn't just leave him. She had her family's support, they'd take her and the kids in, help her get a job, whatever she needed, but she just kept taking the man back.

"You think Mary might end up snapping?" Abe asked.

Scrubbing his hands through his hair Will sighed. "Yeah, I do. Would be a real shame too. After everything he's put her through, I'd hate to see her break and do something that might have her wind up in prison when she's the one who's been victimized for over a decade."

"Not much we can do I guess," Abe said, although his eyes were troubled, no one wanted to see things end that way. "Keep arresting him when we have proof he's hurt Mary or one of the kids. Keep hoping that Mary will see the light."

It didn't feel like enough, but unfortunately it was their only option.

"Yeah," he agreed, heading for his desk.

"Sometimes there's just nothing we can do," Abe called after him.

If that wasn't the story of his life then nothing was. He'd made a mistake and lost the woman that he loved and nothing he had done had changed that. He'd tried calling and emailing several times those first few months, but none of his calls were ever answered, and none of his emails returned, in the end he'd had no choice but to accept that it was over.

Didn't mean he had to like it.

He had hoped that time and distance would help, that one day Renee would realize that even though he'd hurt her, abandoned her, betrayed her, he loved her and if they tried hard enough they could find a way to reclaim what they'd once had.

So far that hadn't happened.

It wasn't likely it ever would.

So why couldn't he let her go?

~

1:37 P.M.

Of course her mom had forgotten something.

And not just something but something important.

With an irritated sigh, Renee stuck her feet into a pair of white flat sandals, straightened the skirt of her pink and white floral sundress, and grabbed her purse. She paused at the last second, her hair was long and thick, reaching down to her bottom, and it was hot outside. If she had to leave the air-conditioned house, then she would have to put it up. Running upstairs, she walked into the bathroom where she had set out her toiletries earlier, grabbed a brush, ran it through her hair, then grabbed a hair donut and put her hair into a bun high on her head. Because she was kind of a sucker for anything cute, she grabbed a pink bow and clipped it under the bun in the bottom left, satisfied she wouldn't expire in the heat in the time it would take to grab a couple of cans of food for the cats.

How could her mother have forgotten that? Half the reason for her coming to stay here—at least from her mom's point of view—was to look after the cats. Her mom had always had a house full of cats for as long as Renee could remember, and while she didn't mind cats, she was definitely more of a dog girl. Maybe she should look into getting a puppy when she went back home, it would be good company in her lonely life, and it would be something to focus on besides the problems she had created for herself.

Back downstairs, she grabbed her purse again and headed out into the heat. This wasn't how she'd expected to spend her day when she arrived here a couple of hours ago. She hadn't wanted to have to head out this soon after being back in town, she'd hoped for a few days to get used to being in River's End again before she saw anyone, but that obviously wasn't going to be the case. Perhaps this was the better option after all, at least she wouldn't spend the next couple of days obsessing over what people were going to say to her.

Driving through the town, she realized this place hadn't changed much since she left. The streets all looked the same, families bustled about enjoying the hot weather and summer vacation, teenagers rode bikes and skateboards and walked in small groups laughing and talking, and she couldn't help but think of how many times she and Will had walked these same streets. They'd been friends even before they'd started dating and they'd hung out often, catching movies, going to the river to swim, dates to the ice cream parlor. They'd spent so much time together that it was hard to believe she hadn't seen or spoken to him in sixteen months.

Unlike the majority of the rest of the stores in town, the supermarket was not on the main street, it was nestled in the suburban area, and that was where she headed now.

Once she parked her car, she took a couple of deep breaths to calm herself. It was ridiculous that she was this nervous about going into a store, but so much of who she was and how she lived her life had changed since she'd been assaulted.

One single second in time could change everything.

It had happened to her.

Gone was that confidence that came with not having come into close contact with the evil in the world.

Now that she had come into contact with it she kept waiting for something else to happen. Every noise could be the footsteps of someone coming to grab her, every corner could be hiding someone, and each time she went to sleep she was making herself vulnerable. Each day was a battle.

A battle she was tired of fighting.

She needed a break.

What she wouldn't give right now to just have five minutes of peace, where she wasn't battling to keep control of her emotions instead of letting them control her. Where she wasn't hyperaware of everything happening around her so that this time she would be ready when danger came for her. Where she wasn't fighting fear and shame and humiliation and loss. She just wanted peace.

Knowing she couldn't sit in the car all afternoon, she'd probably draw attention that way anyway, she opened the door and got out. It was a quick in and out, and really she didn't have to stop and chat, she could always brush people off saying she'd just driven here and put off talking till another day.

Thankfully, the supermarket was quiet, and although she felt a few eyes on her and she saw a few people she recognized no one came up to her. She found the pet food aisle, had no idea which brand her mom used for her cats so she picked one at random and headed for the checkout.

"Renee?"

Looked like her luck had run out. She approached the smiling woman at the checkout. "Hi, Mrs. Russell," she greeted the woman in her sixties who had been working at the supermarket for as long as she could remember.

"I thought it was you." Mrs. Russell beamed. "I didn't know you were back in town."

"I'm not. Well, not really. I'm just housesitting while my mom is away on a cruise," she explained as she set down the cans and the box of dry cat food.

"That's nice. We've missed you around town, been a while since you've been back here. What, about two years?" From the look on the woman's face as she scanned the items, it was clear she was fishing for information on the assault but didn't want to come right out and say it. Well, Renee wasn't in the mood to feed the gossip mill.

"About that," she said vaguely as she handed over her credit card.

Getting the message that she wasn't going to cough up juicy details, Mrs. Russell scanned the card and then handed it back. "Hope to see you again soon, dear."

"I'm sure you will," she said as she picked up her things and headed back outside. That hadn't gone too badly, certainly better than she could have hoped, and she was just starting to feel like she was home free, and all her anxiety had been for nothing when she saw him.

Him.

Will.

Will Black.

Here.

In the parking lot.

She hadn't known that he was back in River's End.

Her feet stopped working, and she stood there staring at the man who had owned her heart from the moment she was old enough to be interested in boys and the woman who was draped all over him.

He'd moved on.

The knowledge was like a physical blow. She felt it hit her stomach and then radiate throughout her body until it consumed her.

Of course he wouldn't stay single for long.

Will was sexy with his reddish-brown hair, his twinkling hazel eyes, his to die for body, and his ability to switch his personality depending on his audience. It was what had made him such a good undercover cop, he was like a chameleon, he could fit in anywhere, make anyone feel like they were the most important person in the world because when he looked at you, it was like he had eyes only for you.

Now here he was with someone else.

No wonder he had stopped trying to contact her.

As irrational as it was—given that she was the one who had ended things—it had hurt when he'd stopped calling and sending emails. It was like he had just given up on her, on them. He could have fought for her, Renee didn't know if it would have made a difference, but it hurt that he hadn't.

She'd been vulnerable, her self-worth shattered, having spent her entire childhood being either fought over or not wanted had messed with her head, shaped her identity, it had made it hard to trust people when even her parents could go hot and cold on her. Then life with Will had been hard, him being away so much, she hadn't realized it at the time, but after he'd left she'd wondered if he'd spent so much time away because deep down he hadn't really wanted to be with her.

Maybe she'd been right.

Maybe her assault was the escape clause Will had been waiting for.

Maybe that was why he had left right afterward.

Fighting back the tears that threatened to escape because she absolutely was not going to cry in the supermarket parking lot and make herself even more of a target for gossip, she was about to flee when he saw her.

Despite sixteen months apart, she could tell the second his gaze was on her, she could feel it. His gaze was like a gentle caress that swept over her body and yanked at her heart, practically begging her to go to him and throw herself into his arms, seek whatever comfort he was willing to give, and soak it up.

She might have done it if it wasn't for the other woman.

Regret, fear, and determination that she was on the right path, the path that protected her already fragile heart, stopped her from making the mistake of going to him and making a fool of herself, and instead she fled for her car.

~

1:54 P.M.

Renee.

Here.

In town.

Standing just fifty yards away.

His first thought was overwhelming relief. Renee was back, and this was the second chance he had been praying for ever since she shut him out of her life.

He would win her back.

As far as Will was concerned, it was already a foregone conclusion.

She'd come back here, she had to know that if she gave him an opening he was going to use it, he'd never wanted to walk away in the first place.

His second thought was that Renee didn't look happy to see him.

She looked sad.

No, she looked downright devastated, like someone had reached into her chest and ripped out her heart.

He knew the feeling.

"Will," a whiny voice dragged his attention away from Renee, and he quickly realized why she was so upset.

Ever since he'd moved back to River's End, there had been a never-ending parade of women interested in dating him—he'd been interested in none of them. Most moved on, there were other eligible bachelors in town, but one in particular had been insistent to the point of making a fool out of herself. Janet Evans had gone to school with him, been in the same class, and had had a crush on him since middle school. That he'd had eyes only for Renee had annoyed Janet and she'd regularly gone out of her way to try to end things between the two of them, bullying Renee and throwing herself at him.

"I have to go, Janet," he said, gently pushing the woman off him.

"But, Will," she whined. "Will I see you later?"

"No." It wasn't like he wanted to be blunt, but so far trying to be tactful hadn't gotten through to Janet.

Turning, the woman saw who had captured his attention. "Oh, *she's* back in town. Tell her to stay away from you, Will. She dumped you, you don't have to put up with her drama anymore. She always was a drama queen."

"Don't you ever say something like that about her again," he growled. He hadn't meant to scare her, but from the way Janet's eyes widened he knew that he had. Renee was all the best pieces of him. She was a sweet, compassionate woman who was always looking for the best in people, she didn't deserve to be spoken about like that, especially since it wasn't true. Renee was the least dramatic woman he'd met.

"Just trying to look out for you." Janet huffed.

Renee had turned and was all but running through the parking lot now. There was no way he was letting her get away, not when he was closer to her than he had been in sixteen long months.

"I don't need you to look out for me, Janet," he said, already moving toward Renee. He caught up to her just as she was shoving a box of cat food into the back of her car. Since he knew she was a dog person, he wondered if she was staying at her mother's house. "Renee."

She let out a startled squawk and dropped what was in her hands as she spun around swinging.

"Hey, it's only me," he soothed, easily deflecting the fist she swung at him.

"Will," she said, breathing heavily as she stared at him as though he were an apparition sprung straight from her nightmares. Was that really how she thought of him? Had he hurt her that badly that she couldn't even stand to look at him?

Her gaze was fixed on his chest, and slowly it lifted to meet his. Emotions swirled through her eyes, and she blinked quickly as though she could hide what she was feeling from him. Too bad he knew her better than anyone else. Hidden in those gorgeous dark eyes of hers he'd seen the one thing he needed to know that he still had a chance with her.

Love.

Renee still loved him, and that filled him with a hope that had been slowly draining out of him with each day he spent apart from her.

Abruptly, she stooped and with shaking hands began to gather up what she'd dropped.

"Here, let me get them," he said. Nudging her gently out of the way, he bent and picked up a couple of cans of cat food. "You staying with your mom?"

"Y-yes," she said hesitantly.

"You back in town for good?" He hardly dared to hope that she might be, if she wasn't, it meant he would have to work quickly to find a way to show how sorry he was for hurting her and earn back her trust.

"No, I needed a break, and Mom and Ben are off on a cruise for the next couple of months. I'm housesitting for them."

Something in the way she'd said she needed a break set off alarm bells. "Needed a break?" he asked, trying to sound nonchalant. "Everything okay?"

"Fine," she said quickly. *Too* quickly.

Something was definitely up, but he let it go for now. If she was upset or worried about something there was no way she would tell him, she didn't trust him. Searching for a way to put her at ease, a way to start building trust again, he held out the cans. "Here you go."

"Thank you," she said softly.

Reaching out to take the cans, despite her careful efforts to avoid touching him, her fingers brushed against his. It might be the briefest of touches but after so long without her that spark that shot between them hit him straight in the heart. From the way she sucked in a breath, Will knew it had affected her too.

"I have to go," she mumbled.

"Renee, wait," he begged. As happy as he was to be standing here face to face with her, he knew the feeling wasn't mutual, but he couldn't let her go just yet. There had to be a way to win her back, but right now he had no idea what that way was. "Please, can we just talk? I know I hurt you, I'm not going to make excuses, I don't want to give you my explanation, I just want to talk."

"I don't think that's a good idea."

"You're here for a couple of months?"

She hesitated, then nodded. "Two."

Two months, that wasn't a lot of time to disassemble the walls that Renee had built, but he'd work with what he had because this time he wasn't letting her go, he would fight for them.

"Are ... do ... umm ... do you live here now?"

"I do, I'm a deputy." Will would take the fact that she was asking as a good sign, it meant she cared enough to want to know.

"When did you move?"

"Sixteen months ago."

Pain flared in her eyes, and she looked at something over his shoulder. Tilting her chin out like she expected a blow, there was a slight tremble in her bottom lip, but she chewed on it to calm it. "So, you and Janet are ...?"

His brow crinkled. Was she seriously asking if he was dating someone else? Did she not know that she was his heart? His soul? Renee was his reason for living. Even if she never took him back he wouldn't get involved with another woman. Reaching for her, he held her shoulders, noting and hating the way she stiffened in his grasp. "Renee, I'm not with Janet or anyone else, not now not ever. I know you don't want to hear this, but I love you, and the only woman I want to be with is you."

Anger flared in her eyes, and he'd take that over the pain any day. "If you wanted to be with me you wouldn't have left. I asked you to stay, *begged* you to stay, and you walked out the door. *You* ruined what we had." She shoved him in the chest, shot him an icy glare, then jumped into her car and drove off.

Will stood looking after her. Their exchange hadn't gone as well as he'd hoped, but then again it hadn't gone as badly as it could have either. She was still angry and hurt, but she cared enough to be upset by the possibility that he might have moved on, and he had to take that to mean that she still loved him.

When she had ended things sixteen months ago, she'd told him that sometimes love wasn't enough and that without trust, there was nothing to build a foundation on. Will was determined to rebuild that foundation, he'd do anything that Renee needed him to do to earn her trust back, he knew he'd messed up, made a mistake, but he had to believe that the fact they loved each other meant that it was possible. And if it was possible then he could make it happen.

"I love you, Renee, and I'm going to prove it to you so we can have the life we were supposed to have."

CHAPTER
Five

August 3rd
8:50 A.M.

"We should have known that it would end this way," Will said as he stared at the body.

It had been inevitable, only a matter of time, and yet that didn't stop him from feeling guilty. They should have done something to prevent it, worked harder, and been smarter. Looking back, there were so many what-if moments that could have changed this outcome, and yet at the same time, deep down he knew there was nothing anyone could have done to change this.

Raphael Russo had been too far gone. His anger combined with alcohol abuse meant that he was a ticking time bomb and nothing would diffuse him.

Didn't mean this was easy.

"Any chance this could be something else than an abusive partner losing it?" he asked his friend and fellow deputy, Fletcher Harris.

"Always a chance that things aren't as they seem," Fletcher replied.

"Why? Are you thinking something doesn't add up? That it wasn't Raphael who killed Mary?"

"Why not just stab her, or shoot her? This seems like an odd way for him to have killed her if he wanted her out of the picture," he replied. It wasn't that he thought someone else had killed Mary Pino, he was sure this was the work of her husband. They already knew the man had been abusing her for years, it was just that it seemed too elaborate.

"He wanted her to suffer," Fletcher said simply.

He wasn't wrong.

Mary Pino had a rope around her neck, and the other end of the rope had been tied to a metal pole which had been fixed between two corners of the room, right up near the ceiling. The rope was short enough that Mary would have been able to reach the pole to hold on to it, but depending on how long she was left there, eventually her arms would have given out, no longer able to hold her body weight. Once that happened she would have asphyxiated as the rope cut off her air supply.

It would have been a long and terrifying death.

She would probably have lost and reclaimed her grip a couple of times before exhaustion had claimed her and she hadn't been able to hold on any longer.

"How long do you think she could have lasted?" Fletcher asked.

"A while, hours maybe. Since she was fighting for her life, she would have given it everything she had." Will was positive of that, but the facts were no one could hold up their own bodyweight indefinitely with only their arms.

"You think he watched?"

"I think if you go to this much trouble to kill someone, then yeah, you hang around to watch until they're dead."

"What did he do with the kids while he did this?" Fletcher asked. "I've been out here before, and there was no pole in the ceiling, so he had to come here, subdue Mary somehow, then fix the pole, and then get her up there. That would have taken a while and would have been noisy since he had to screw the pole to the walls. There's no way Mary and the kids wouldn't have known he was here and what he was doing.

Seven kids, oldest is almost eleven, youngest is two, that's a lot of kids to keep under control for a really long time."

"I was here the night before last, and there was no pole. He started this sometime yesterday, hopefully we can narrow that down once we get a time of death. When was the last time anyone saw Raphael? We're going to have to try to get a timeline going. We also need to try to figure out where he's going next. If he has the kids with him then it's only a matter of time before someone is going to spot him. He's going to have to buy food, diapers. If he's traveling, there will be frequent bathroom stops. If he's holed up somewhere, he's going to have to let them outdoors at some point, no way he can handle all seven of them inside indefinitely. And that's assuming they're cooperating. I know that Ken has really been standing up for his mom, so if he knows what his dad did then there's no way he's going to sit there quietly."

"He might not have the kids with him," Fletcher said slowly, flexing his shoulder where he'd been shot two months ago. He'd worked hard at his physical therapy, but Will knew the joint still bothered him.

"You think he killed them too?" As much as he hated the idea it was definitely a possibility. "We should check out the house and property, see what we find."

"I'll check inside, you check outside," Fletcher suggested.

With a nod, he headed out of the ramshackle house into the overgrown yard. The property was around four acres, most of it forest. There were any number of places he could have hidden the bodies, especially if he'd been planning this for some time. They would do a more thorough search later, but for now, he'd just look for any place where there was recently disturbed earth.

As he walked the property, methodically moving horizontally from left to right up and down, scanning side to side as he went, he couldn't help but have his thoughts stray to Renee. Knowing she was so close, his house was just six blocks from Renee's mother's house where she was staying, and yet he couldn't touch her, hold her, kiss her, was torture. He wanted her so badly it hurt. Being away from Renee was like dying a slow death from a virus that had no cure. He'd heard of people dying from a broken heart, and that was what he felt was happening to him.

Every day he lost a little piece of himself. Those pieces weren't physical, they were his soul.

He'd done things in his time as a SEAL, and in his time undercover that ate away at him, they'd been the right thing to do in the moment, but that didn't mean he liked them. He didn't deserve someone like Renee, and yet she loved him, and what had he done with that love? He'd thrown it back in her face and walked out the door like it meant nothing to him. Maybe the right thing to do was walk away, he'd hurt her enough, but he was selfish enough to know he could never leave her. He had to fight for her. For them.

Was he really any better than Raphael Russo?

Raphael had hurt the woman he claimed to love, and he'd done the same thing. Renee had been raped, she'd been traumatized, she'd no doubt had nightmares, flashbacks, she'd lost her sense of safety, she'd probably become hyper-vigilant, scared to be alone, the very foundation of her world rocked. He'd made it worse by making her go through it alone. When they had first gotten together, he promised her that she would be the most important thing in his life and he hadn't followed through on that promise.

In his mind, he'd done the same thing to Renee that Raphael had to Mary. Hurting someone was hurting someone, it didn't matter how you did it, the end result was the same.

Finding nothing that indicated bodies had recently been dumped out here, he headed back to the house. If the kids were still alive, he didn't think they were in any immediate danger from their father. If Raphael had wanted them dead then he would have killed them when he killed Mary.

First thing they'd do when they finished up here would be to speak with Mary's parents and find out when they'd last seen the kids. If they were really lucky, maybe the kids were safe and sound at their grandparents' house.

Informing the Pinos that their daughter was dead was not something he was looking forward to. He'd done his fair share of family notifications since he'd moved back to River's End. The majority had been related to car accidents, or the occasional skiing or boating accident, and every time he did one he couldn't help but think of Renee. He'd been the one to find her so it wasn't like he'd had cops approach him and inform him that she'd been attacked, but he remembered standing in the hospital corridor calling her family and breaking the news of what had happened as gently as he could.

Everything in his life related back to Renee in some way.

He didn't know any other way to live.

She was his other half, and seeing her yesterday was like being given a second chance at life. He would win her back, and he was already working on a plan to make it happen. Will had to believe that it would work, he had to believe that if he could just remind Renee of how good things between them had been, and how sorry he was for hurting her that he could earn her trust enough for her to give him a second chance.

11:32 A.M.

This was why she had offered to housesit for her mother.

Sitting here, on the edge of the river, her bare feet dangling into the cool, crystal clear water, her back resting against the sturdy trunk of an old tree, Renee felt more relaxed than she had in a long time. Sunlight shone down, warming her with a soothing touch that brought peace and tranquility she hadn't been able to find anywhere else these last two years.

Renee had fair skin, and she'd lathered on the sunblock this morning before leaving for the river, but she hoped she developed a little bit of a tan. That was one of her goals for this summer vacation. She wanted to get a bit of color back in her skin, lose the pale white that always had people asking if she felt okay. She'd always had this kind of fair skin, inherited from her mother, and as a kid it had never bothered her, she'd just made sure to cover up and use plenty of sunblock so she didn't burn. She hadn't spent her summers in a bikini with the other girls who'd wanted to lie on their towels and work on their tans, instead she'd spent them swimming, learning to dive, kayaking, water skiing, just enjoying the water.

Okay, so maybe she had worn the bikini while doing that.

She glanced down at herself, this was the first time she'd worn a bikini since her assault. Although they were nothing but a flimsy barrier between her body and the rest of the world, and certainly nothing that had protected her that day, she didn't feel comfortable with anyone seeing too much of her skin. To work, she wore long sleeve blouses and skirts that reached her ankles, boots most of the time, even in summer, and at home she'd stick with sweatpants and sweatshirts, turning up the AC if her clothes weren't appropriate for the season.

Today felt different somehow.

When she'd gotten out of bed this morning, the first thing she'd wanted to do was head out to the river, soak up some rays, read a book, or simply sit and enjoy nature. She hadn't even realized that she'd put on the bikini until it was already on, and although she had initially debated with herself removing it in favor of a sundress that reached her ankles and a cardigan, she had realized she was ready to take this step.

Renee wasn't sure what had brought about the change in her, but she'd passed the two-year mark a couple of days ago, and maybe she had just reached the next stage in getting her life back.

Or it was ...

No.

She had promised herself that she wasn't going to think about Will Black anymore. This trip was about escaping the mess her life was in, getting away from everything and everyone. It was about sitting by the river, going swimming, watching old movies, reading, and trying to relax and rejuvenate.

It was *not* about Will.

If she'd known he was back in River's End, she wouldn't have offered to come back here and stay in her mom's house while she was away. It was too hard being this close to him. Knowing that he was just a few blocks away when she'd climbed into bed last night had been enough to keep her tossing and turning for hours before she'd fallen into a restless slumber.

Why did he have to be here?

Why did he have to say that he still loved her?

Why did he have to say that he wanted her back?

Why couldn't he just leave her alone?

Didn't he know how hard it was for her to see him?

She loved him, would *always* love him, but that wasn't enough. She didn't trust him, and she couldn't rely on him. Even if she could forgive him for hurting her, how could they ever be together?

Was his plan just to use these two months to wear her down until she gave in and took him back? Because if that was his plan, he would find himself sorely disappointed. She wasn't stupid, he'd shown her what kind of man he was, that he couldn't be relied upon to be there when she needed him, and she wasn't going to believe him. Actions spoke louder than words.

So why couldn't her traitorous body get on board?

Just brushing her fingers across his when she'd taken the cans from his hand had been enough for her body to hum with need and desire. She hadn't felt like that since before her attack. Even all the nights she'd laid awake missing Will and the showers where she'd curled up on the floor and cried her eyes out. All the things that had reminded her of him, such as packing up his clothes and belongings when she sold the house, not once in all the times she'd thought of him in two years had she ever missed anything to do with their intimate relationship.

It was like the rape had just turned her body off sex.

It was normal, natural, something she'd work through in her own time and know when she was ready to take that step again her therapist had told her many times, but she hadn't really believed the woman.

Now, it was all she could do not to track Will down and demand he take her to bed.

He owed her, right?

One night of no strings attached hot sex, get him out of her system once and for all and then maybe they could both find closure and move on.

No, that wasn't her.

She didn't do meaningless sex, and Will was the only guy she'd ever been with. As much as she was hurt and angry with him, she couldn't ruin what they'd shared by ending it like that.

With a sigh, she picked up a daisy that was growing nearby and began to pull off the petals. "He loves me, he loves me not, he loves me ..." she broke off the silly childhood chant when she heard voices.

Someone was coming.

Multiple someones.

Renee hated that her first thought was danger. This was River's End, in the height of the summer tourist season, whoever was coming was either locals or holidaymakers here to enjoy the river, not anyone meaning her any harm.

Still, the tranquility of the place was ruined for her now, and she stood, slipping her cotton long-sleeved blouse on and pulling on a pair of denim shorts. She was just shoving her feet into her flip-flops when she saw four women approach. All were wearing bathing suits, and one had a baby in her arms.

Not in the mood to make small talk, she kept her head down and mumbled a greeting as she hurried past them back to her car.

"Renee?"

She froze at the sound of her name, wishing that they had been holidaymakers here to enjoy the river because she didn't want to face questions about what she was doing back in town and how she was doing.

Reluctantly, she lifted her head. She couldn't be rude and brush these women off even if she wanted to. When she looked at the four, she immediately recognized Maggie Wilson, with her long, curly hair, and a woman with shorter brown curls as Poppy Deveraux. Maggie was another River's End resident who had grown up here, they'd known each other their whole lives. Since Maggie was just a year younger than her, they had gone to school together, played together as children, and been friends as teenagers. Poppy had moved to town when she was twelve along with her parents. She was two years younger than Renee but close enough in age that they had also been friends when they were teens.

"Hi, Maggie." She summoned up a smile. "Poppy."

"I didn't know you were back in town." Maggie smiled back.

"Just housesitting for my mom," she said, fighting the urge to squirm. The other two women were looking at her curiously, and she got the feeling that although she didn't know them they knew her, or at least of her.

"This is Will's Renee?" the blonde asked.

"I dropped the Will when we broke up," she shot back dryly before she could stop herself.

The blonde laughed. "I like her already. I'm Meadow. Abe and I are married, and this is our daughter Dawn," she said, indicating the baby asleep in her arms.

"You're married to Abe?" she asked, surprised. Somehow she couldn't see the big, gruff man married with an infant daughter.

Meadow laughed again. "I get that response a lot. Abe is just a big cuddly teddy bear, only he doesn't want anyone to know."

Renee couldn't help but chuckle at the idea. "It's nice to meet you, Meadow."

"I'm Sydney." The fourth woman held out her hand. "I only moved here two months ago. I'm the new deputy, and I'm, umm, dating Levi," she said and blushed.

"Nice to meet you, Sydney. And Levi is a sweetheart, I'm glad he found someone." A diamond glinted in the sunshine, and Renee noticed that Maggie was wearing an engagement ring. "Who's the lucky guy?"

"It's Theo," Maggie said with a dreamy smile. "We're getting married this Christmas, and we're having a baby," she said, resting a hand on her stomach.

She knew a little of Maggie's past, and she was glad that the woman had found happiness. "So you three are going to be sisters-in-law," she said, trying to keep a smile on her face. She was happy for them and Will's cousins, but their happiness only served to remind her that at one time she'd thought that Will's cousins would be part of her family. Only things hadn't turned out that way.

"Yep, one day," Meadow beamed. "We just gotta get Levi to propose to Syd."

"Meadow," Sydney groaned. "He'll do it when he's ready, I don't want to push him."

"Push him, yeah," Poppy said with an accompanying eye roll. "That man doesn't have to be pushed to do anything when it comes to you."

"Are you involved with anyone, Poppy?" Renee asked politely. She had about reached her quota of lovers for the day, but couldn't not ask.

"I am," Poppy said and couldn't wipe the smile off her face. "I met him a few months ago when I went to California to bury my parents. His name is Beau Caldwell, and he moved here with me. He's a cop and transferred to join the Sheriff's office."

"I'm sorry about your parents, but happy you met someone," Renee said.

"Thanks," Poppy said, and it was clear she wanted to ask about Renee's love life, but she prayed that none of the women did.

Renee gave the four women a sad smile, it was nice to see how close they were. She'd basically shut out all of her friends since her assault. She couldn't stand to be betrayed by someone else so she'd pushed them all away before they could leave her too.

As though sensing her sadness, Maggie said, "Why don't you come hang out with us for a while?"

No. She wasn't in the market for new friends, and besides, she was only here for a couple of months. "Uh, thanks, but I have to get going."

"You here for a while?" Poppy asked.

"A couple of months."

"Well, that's plenty of time to catch up. I'd love to know what you've been up to since you left River's End." Maggie beamed at her.

Since it was Maggie and the woman was a total sweetheart, Renee knew she didn't mean any harm, but she also knew that curiosity would get the best of her, and sooner or later the topic of her assault would come up. It was days like today that she wished she hadn't grown up in a small town where your business became everyone's business whether you wanted it to or not.

Feigning a smile, she said, "Sure, sounds great. Gotta go. Enjoy the river."

As she fled for her car, Renee knew that she would avoid any catch-ups at all costs. It was better to be lonely than to give anyone else the power to hurt her by leaving.

~

2:44 P.M.

. . .

More nervous than he should be, Will parked his car outside Renee's mother's house.

He'd always been someone who took fear and anxiety in his stride, as a kid there hadn't been much that had scared him. He'd been in more firefights than he could remember on dozens of SEAL missions, but always been spurred on by the knowledge he was doing something important with his life to even notice fear most of the time. Working undercover was about adopting a character and living as that person if you didn't want to die, focusing on his role hadn't left a lot of time for him to worry about what could go wrong.

The most terrifying moment of his life was when he walked into his and Renee's house that night and realized something was wrong but hadn't yet known if Renee was okay.

The second most terrifying moment of his life was right this second.

Losing Renee was the worst thing that had ever happened to him. He would gladly walk into an ambush, alone, unarmed, then go through that again. All he had thought about for the last sixteen months was how he could get her back, and now he had a chance.

One chance.

That was all he had.

If he messed this up then he would lose her forever.

One mistake and everything he wanted would slip through his fingers.

Gathering the courage that had helped him function in every dangerous situation he'd ever walked into but now seemed to evade him, Will grabbed the bags from the back of his truck and walked up the front path.

Balancing the bags, he knocked, then waited impatiently for Renee to answer. Seconds ticked by with excruciating slowness and he started to wonder if maybe she wasn't home, or if she was taking a nap or a shower, when finally the door was thrown open.

Renee's dark eyes grew wide when she saw him standing there, then immediately they grew suspicious. "Will, what are you doing here?"

Shooting her the most winning smile he could muster, he replied, "Brought you some groceries."

Her brow crinkled. "You brought me groceries? Why?"

"Well, I guessed that you probably weren't up to all the questions you know people are going to have for you, and I know your mom can be a bit of an airhead. You went out yesterday to get cat food, but I bet you didn't bother to get anything for yourself." While that was all true of course the main reason he was here was that it had seemed like a good excuse to come and see her, and right now he wasn't above using any excuse he could scrounge up.

With eyes still narrowed, she hadn't taken a step back to let him into the house, but the first words out of her mouth weren't telling him to get off her mom's property so he had to take that as a positive. "I told you that I don't want to talk."

"You did," he agreed. "I have milk in here and some other perishables, it's hot as Hell out here. You want to let me in so we can put them in the fridge?"

"If you know I don't want to talk to you, then why are you here? Is it really just to bring me groceries?" She crossed her arms across her chest and glared at him, and damn if she didn't look adorably sexy when she pouted like that.

"Babe, right about now as desperate as I am to see you I'd sink low enough to do pretty much anything, but I'm just here to help." Okay, so that was a teeny, tiny, white lie but it was for a good cause, and as a bonus, he really was helping her out.

Renee studied him for a long moment, long enough that he was sure she would slam the door in his face, but then she sighed and stepped back. "Okay then, thank you I guess."

It took everything he had not to cheer at his success.

Progress.

She led him through to the kitchen, and even though he'd been here before and knew his way around he stayed behind her, content to just soak up the sight of her. She looked good, but she was much thinner than when they'd been together, and he had to assume it was because the stress and trauma of her assault had stolen her appetite. Other than that, her hair was a little longer than it had been when he'd last seen her, her skin was a little paler, and she still looked just as sexy in a pair of short shorts that showed off her long legs.

In the kitchen, he set the bags down on the counter and Renee began to unpack them, steadfastly refusing to look his way. That was fine. He knew that she was uncomfortable in his presence because there was so much still unresolved between them, but the only way to get back to that comfortable companionship was to start spending time together.

It took them about five minutes to get everything put away in the fridge and the cupboards and then they stood awkwardly side by side.

"You bought all my favorites," Renee said quietly, breaking the silence that was growing more oppressive by the second.

"Of course," he agreed like it was obvious.

"You still remember everything I loved." She sounded surprised by that, and he realized just how badly he'd hurt her when he'd left if she thought he could forget anything about her.

"Honey, I remember every single thing about you. Every. Single. Thing. I remember how you cut your grapes into quarters because you don't like the way they squirt in your mouth if you eat them whole. I remember that you change the bed linens every single day because you love the feel of fresh sheets when you climb into bed at night. I remember how you drink your coffee with more milk than coffee because you like the caffeine but not the taste of coffee. I remember the way you screw up that cute little nose of yours when you're concentrating. I remember the way you chew on your bottom lip right before you scream my name when you come. Renee." He put one hand on her shoulder to turn her to face him and hooked his forefinger under her chin, nudging gently so she stopped staring at the center of his chest and looked him in the eye instead. "I love you, and when I left it wasn't because I didn't want to be there for you. I *ached* to be the one to hold you, comfort you, tell you everything would be okay, but I thought you needed him caught. I was wrong, what you needed was me. I'll be sorry about not being there for you every day for the rest of my life."

"*You* needed him caught, I just needed you." Anger flared in her face, but then it died away. "I don't want to sound like a broken record saying that over and over again. What's done is done, it's over, we can't go back, I think it's best that we just keep our distance while I'm here."

"I can't do that," he said honestly, letting his fingers caress her jaw. "I love you, and I don't want to let you go."

"You already did."

"The biggest mistake of my life." Will prayed she understood that hurting her had been the last thing he'd wanted to do.

"I don't want to give you false hope," she warned. "Don't go getting any thoughts of us getting back together in that thick head of yours. Being all sweet and helpful and bringing me groceries isn't going to change anything, that ship has sailed."

"You think I'm sweet?" he asked with a grin. Never in his life before this moment had he ever wanted a woman, especially one he was in love with, to describe him as sweet. Strong, tough, protective, he was all of those things, but sweet was the equivalent of cute in his mind, and this former SEAL, ex-undercover agent was not cute in any way, shape, or form.

Renee rolled her eyes at him, but her lips quirked up in a smile, the first smile he'd seen from her since before she was assaulted. "Don't go letting that head of yours get any bigger."

"Too late." He grinned.

"Look, Will, I don't want to be angry anymore. You hurt me when you left like you did, hurt me in a way I didn't even know I could be hurt, I can't give you power over me to do that again, but maybe one day we could be friends."

Curling an arm around her waist, Will drew her up close so she was pressed right up against his chest. "Renee, the two of us can never be *just* friends. We're soul mates, two halves of a whole, destined to be together. If you give me a chance, I'll earn your trust back, and then we can get back what we lost because I am not walking away from you ever again. Ever."

With that, he dipped his head and whispered his lips across hers then he released her and turned and walked away. He would win Renee back. She'd been his lighthouse for so long, calling him back from the darkest places that he had been, guiding him through internal storms that could have dashed him against the rocks, shone so brightly that even everything he had done couldn't black out his spirit.

Now she needed him to be her lighthouse, guide her back through the storms so she came out safely on the other side.

He'd do that for her if she let him.

~

3:03 P.M.

Her lips burned as though they'd been branded.

Renee stood staring at the closed front door for a good five minutes before she was able to rouse herself enough to function and form a coherent thought.

Why did Will have to do that?

Why did he have to be all sweet and thoughtful? Bringing her groceries so she wouldn't have to go out and face questions from nosy—even if they mostly meant well—people because he knew she wouldn't be up for that.

Why did he have to tell her that he thought they were soul mates, two halves of a whole, destined to be together?

And why did he have to kiss her? Was he trying to confuse her?

Feeling drained, Renee left the kitchen and dragged herself into the living room where she dropped down into a corner of the sofa. One of the cats immediately came to jump onto her lap, and she absently stroked the soft, silky fur. It felt like the rocky foundation she had been rebuilding her life on these last two years had just suffered a major crack.

A crack she wasn't sure she knew how to fix.

"He left *me* you know," she told the cat, who purred loudly as she scratched it behind it's ears.

Will had walked away even though she'd asked him not to, and he'd done it at the very worst time in her life. He'd betrayed her, abandoned her, left her to deal with something so horrendous that it had marred every fiber of her being. If he could do that then, how could he say that he had ever loved her?

In those first few weeks and months after her assault, she had dedicated many an hour to trying to figure out how he could do it. She had convinced herself that she had been wrong all along and what she'd thought they had obviously hadn't been real. Because when you loved someone you were there for them at the lowest points of their lives, you didn't up and leave to satisfy your own needs.

Will had effectively ended things when he left, so why did he now want to start things back up between them?

What did it mean?

And why did she care?

Renee had promised herself when she was learning to rebuild her life, learning to be strong again, that she would never ever allow anyone to have the power to hurt her the way Will had. There was no way she wanted to go back down this route with Will because the bottom line was that even if the anger faded, and even though she still loved him, she didn't trust him, and that meant that nothing could ever work out with them.

So why couldn't she forget that kiss?

And why did it leave her body burning for more?

She had enough going on in her life to keep her busy so there was no reason she should be obsessing over this. Coming here was an escape. Yeah, it was a break and a chance to get some much-needed rest and relaxation, but basically it was to get away from her life for a while and from the mistakes that she had made.

Mistakes that still ate at her.

Mistakes that she could never rectify.

Mistakes that she knew were going to result in people being hurt.

All because she hadn't seen the truth.

It had been staring her in the face, and yet she hadn't seen it. She'd believed the best in him, but she had been so very wrong. Obviously, she wasn't very good at reading people. She'd misread her relationship with Will and now this.

"I'm not going to cry over him again," she told the cat, forcing back the tears that pricked at the backs of her eyes. She'd cried enough for an entire lifetime, and she'd long since decided that there was no man on the face of the earth worth shedding more over.

Okay, she roused herself, this wasn't productive.

This was a vacation, one she'd intended to catch up on some much-needed sleep and to chill out. Obsessing over past mistakes and past relationships was never going to achieve that.

Maggie, Poppy, and their friends had asked her to hang out with them. She'd said no because at the time she hadn't wanted to be around anyone, but being alone wasn't proving to be very helpful either, so maybe hanging out with others was the answer. She'd known Maggie basically her whole life and Poppy since she was a teen —both women were sweet. She couldn't see either of them pumping her for information, and maybe catching up on each other's lives and getting to know some new people would be the distraction she needed so she could stop thinking about Will and that kiss. That darn kiss had her body humming with a need she hadn't experienced in a long time.

Standing up, the cat gave an irritated meow but immediately curled up and went back to sleep when she set it on the chair she'd just vacated, Renee stretched her tired, tight muscles, and headed back into the kitchen where she'd left her phone. She didn't have Maggie's number or Poppy's, and she wouldn't be calling the precinct to try to catch Poppy because she didn't want to risk getting Will instead, but she could call the hotel that Maggie owned and speak to her there, or leave her number and a message and let the other woman call her back.

As she picked up her phone her gaze lingered on the box of donuts that Will had brought her. There wasn't a chocolate one in the box, he'd obviously remembered that she was allergic to chocolate and loved strawberry icing best of all because every single one of them had pink icing.

He was so thoughtful.

Even when they'd been together he'd been like that. They hadn't had a lot of time together, but what time they had spent together Will had always made sure to make the most of it—breakfasts in bed, picnics, lazy evenings lying with her head in his lap binge-watching shows. He caught up on chores around the house so she wouldn't have to do them, cooked her dinners—always her favorites—took her on fun dates, and although he could definitely be an alpha through and through, he *always* encouraged her to talk to him about anything and everything that was on her mind.

Maybe that was why it had hurt so badly when he left.

She'd trusted him with her whole heart, believed that he would never hurt her, never betray her trust, but in hindsight, she wondered if she had just been seeing what she wanted to see. After all, he spent more time away from her than he did with her, if that wasn't an indication of how serious he saw their relationship, then she didn't know what was.

"Renee, come on," she admonished herself aloud. "You know that obsessing over him is only going to cause you more pain. Are you a masochist or something? Is that what you want? More pain? Haven't you had enough?"

Her little pep talk worked, and she forced herself to shove away those thoughts. She knew what it was like to ride the Will seesaw, she'd done it enough in the early months, wavering between caving and begging him to come to her because she needed his strength, and determination to let him go because he'd hurt her and she could find a way to be strong on her own. There was no way she was getting back on that ride.

Just as she was about to find the number for Maggie's hotel her phone buzzed with a text.

Immediate dread filled her at the thought it could be someone from her office. Her boss hadn't been happy that she'd taken her vacation time now, but that was because he didn't know the mess she'd made of the last case she'd worked.

When she looked at the screen her heart stopped.

The message wasn't from work, it was from Will.

How did he even get her number?

And why did the text show up with his name?

Had he somehow managed to sneak his phone number into her phone when they'd been unloading the groceries?

Sneaky little thing.

Will
Hey, Little Bird, thinking of you
Can't get that kiss out of my head
Next time we do that my lips won't only be on yours
they'll be feasting on every inch of your beautiful body
You can fight it but we're meant to be together
Sooner or later fate will throw us back together
I love you and I'm sorry for hurting you

Somehow I'll make it up to you, that's a promise

He was awfully cocky for a guy who had just been told in no uncertain terms that she didn't want to get back together with him. He was so confident that he could make things up to her, earn her trust back, and he was already planning what would happen next.

Why did his attitude and his words leave her body tingling and her defenses softening? It didn't help that he used the nickname he'd had for her when they were kids. She had a habit of singing quietly to herself when she was doing things, and he'd joked that she was like a bird always chirping away, and the nickname had stuck.

She didn't want to get back with him, and him acting like it was already a foregone conclusion should make her angry, and yet she couldn't deny that excitement mixed with longing was filling her heart right now.

To reply or not to reply, that was the question.

She knew it wasn't wise to encourage him, and yet he was trying so hard, and maybe this was what she had needed sixteen months ago. For him to fight for her—for them—rather than giving up and walking away.

This was no doubt a mistake, but she couldn't seem to help herself.

Renee
Thank you for the donuts
I'll think of you when I'm eating them

Less than five seconds later, dots appeared indicating he was typing out a reply.

Will
Babe, now I'm imaging your lips on *my* body

How am I going to focus on work now?!

She giggled despite herself.

Renee
Sorry!

Will
Not buying it
But you will be sorry when my tongue is
teasing every inch of you
Soon, babe, I promise you that
Soon I'll be reminding you just how
perfect our bodies are together
How perfect *we* are together

Heat pooled low in her stomach, and she knew that she was playing with fire and that she would get burned, she just couldn't make herself care enough to stop.

~

9:17 P.M.

"Will, we found him."

He looked up from his phone, the smile on his face dying when he saw his brother standing in the doorway. The perfect afternoon this had turned into, texting with Renee, seeing her start to let her guard down a little, let him in, was clearly over.

"Raphael?" he asked Julian. It was the only major case they were working right now so he couldn't think of anyone else his brother would be talking about.

"Mr. Higgsly saw him out on the old Fromyer farm. After Mrs. Fromyer passed away two years ago the place has been sitting there empty, it's quiet and secluded, the perfect place for him to hide out. If Mr. Higgsly's goat hadn't gotten loose and he hadn't had to go tracking through the forest looking for it, there's no telling how long he could have hidden out there."

"We all heading there?"

"Yes. Abe already called Fletcher, Beau, and Sydney, they're heading out now."

Will nodded. After his brief visit to Renee's earlier this afternoon, he, Julian, and Abe had been doing everything they could to track Raphael down, knowing that if the kids were with him that they were in danger. According to Mary's parents, the last time they had seen their daughter was when she picked up her kids from their place early yesterday morning, meaning the kids had almost definitely been at the house when their father killed their mother.

There had been no sign of any of the seven of them since.

He hoped that was because their father had taken them with him and not because they were dead already.

"Mr. Higgsly see any of the kids?" he asked.

"No, just saw Raphael sitting on the front porch drinking."

"All right, meet you in the car in thirty seconds," he said, dismissing his brother.

Julian cocked his head and arched a brow but didn't say anything and headed out of the office, letting the door swing closed behind him.

Picking his phone back up, he sent Renee a quick text. This wasn't how he'd wanted to end things tonight, he'd hoped to keep up the easy banter until he went to bed, but duty called. He and Renee had been texting all afternoon, any time he tried to broach the subject of them as a couple and their past and the future they could have, she veered the topic back toward something neutral, but at least she was softening toward him, and he knew she was thinking about that kiss as much as he was.

It hadn't been a conscious decision, he'd just kissed her because it was Renee, the love of his life, and there was only so long he could spend in her presence without touching her. But he meant it when he'd said he wouldn't put his lips on her again until she asked him to. It had to be her call. If they had any shot at a second chance it had to come from her. She had to find a way to forgive him.

Will
Hey, babe, I gotta go, duty calls
I wish I could hear you sing yourself
to sleep tonight, Little Bird

He watched the little dots indicating she was replying as though they were his lifeline. That she was responding to his texts was better than he could have hoped for this soon after fate had tossed them back into the same town.

Renee
Okay, stay safe

Will
I will
Sweet dreams, Little Bird

Renee
Goodnight, Will, sweet dreams

Will
Oh my dreams will be sweet, Little Bird

I'll be dreaming about you
I really have to go now,
I'll talk to you tomorrow
Love you, sweetheart

Renee
Goodnight

She didn't return his sentiment, but that was okay, he knew that she loved him, she'd told him she did. It was trusting him again that was the problem. And as a bonus, she hadn't argued about him texting again tomorrow. That was a definite win.

Shoving his phone into his pocket, he grabbed his gun, holstered it, then hurried out to join Abe and Julian. He wished that he could go home to Renee tonight, climb into bed and pull her soft body into his arms, listen to her sing herself to sleep in that sweet way she did, then fall asleep knowing that the woman he loved was safe. Soon. He prayed that soon that wish would become a reality. He had to push but not too hard, fight for them, take small steps, and be content with the progress that he made and not expect too much too soon.

"What's the plan?" he asked as he slipped into the back seat of Abe's truck.

"Fletcher, Sydney, and Beau are going to come in from the back of the property, through the McCall place. We're going to go in the front, we'll split up, try to establish whether the children are there and what their condition is before we go in. Equal priority is getting Raphael in custody and ensuring the kids' safety," Abe said as he started driving.

In the twenty minutes it took them to drive, they coordinated with the others exactly how this was all going to go down, and by the time Abe was parking the truck out the front of the old Fromyer place, Will was firmly in the zone.

"I'll go down the drive, Will you circle around and come in from the left, Julian you take the right," Abe gave the orders as they all climbed out of the vehicle.

The place was heavily forested, and the house wasn't visible from the road, Raphael wouldn't know they were coming until they were practically on him. Mr. Higgsly had seen him drinking so if they were lucky the man was passed out and they could safely remove the kids and get him in handcuffs before he had a chance to do anything stupid. And Will had a feeling that Raphael was currently sitting at rock bottom. As far as he was concerned there was nothing left to lose, and he wouldn't hesitate to take out one of his kids if he thought it would work to his advantage.

He was halfway to the house when he heard the sounds of branches rustling and twigs snapping.

Someone was coming.

Focusing on the details, he noted that it was more than one person and that whoever it was was small, too small to be Raphael.

He took a few steps in the direction of the sounds and a moment later nine-year-old Vanessa Russo, Raphael and Mary's second child, came into view. In her arms she carried the youngest sibling, two-year-old Timmy, and four-year-old twins, Eva and Greg were right on her heels.

When she caught sight of him, Vanessa let out a shrill scream and tried to bolt. Given that she was a scrawny little thing and already weighed down with a toddler in her arms, he was easily able to pull her into his arms.

"It's okay, Vanessa, it's Will Black, you're safe now, okay? You're all safe," he soothed while scanning the area for the other kids. He didn't see them, which meant that five-year-old Sarah, seven-year-old Orlando, and ten-year-old Duke were all still in the house with their father. "I want you to take your siblings and go to the road. The sheriff's truck is parked there. I want you to get in, lock the doors, and keep down out of sight, okay?"

The child was shaking in his arms, but she nodded bravely. "Are you going to get Sarah, Orlando, and Duke away from Daddy?" she asked.

"We're going to do everything we can to make sure that all of you get home safely," he promised.

"Daddy hurt Mommy," the girl said, starting to cry.

"I know, baby. Your Grandma and Grandpa will take good care of you though. You good to go?"

The child dragged in a deep breath then nodded. Shifting the weight of her baby brother, she looked for the twins. "You two hold onto my dress, okay?"

The terrified little ones nodded, and Will watched until the children had disappeared from view. That was four of the kids safe but three still in danger, and if Raphael realized that four of his children had managed to escape there was no telling how he would react.

Confident that Vanessa could do as he'd instructed and get herself and her younger siblings to safety, he continued on toward the house. The second he approached it he knew that the children's escape hadn't gone unnoticed.

"Where are they?" Raphael was screaming, presumably at the remaining kids.

When there was no reply the sound of splintering wood could be heard.

"I'm not going to ask you again, boy. Where did your sister go?"

Will reached the side of the house and peeked through a grimy window. Inside there was enough light for him to be able to see that the five and seven-year-old were huddled together in a corner, while ten-year-old Duke stood straight and tall in the middle of his father's wrath.

Abe was at the front door, he had no doubt that Sydney, Beau, and Fletcher were at the back, so he quietly slipped across the dilapidated porch and joined Abe as Julian also approached them.

"Vanessa and the three youngest are in the car," he whispered to let the others know what was going on.

His cousin gave a single nod before they breached the house, guns drawn.

They headed straight for the kitchen on the left where Raphael and the kids were.

"Raphael, down on the floor, hands on your head," Abe yelled at the man.

Turning slowly, swaying on his feet, Raphael grabbed Duke and dragged him up close, using the boy—who had a black eye and a bloody cheek—as a human shield. Raphael didn't have a weapon on him, other than his fists, but with the kid in front of him none of them could get off a shot. "Get outta here." The man's slurred speech was a sure indication he was drunk. "This not noneya bisness. Family bisness."

"You're not walking out of that door in any other way but in handcuffs, Raphael," Abe said, voice calm and collected.

"Sarah, Orlando, go on outside," Will told the crying children as he slowly circled the room toward them.

Two sets of terrified eyes darted between him and the drunk man in the middle of the room.

"It's okay," he assured them. "Off you go, now."

Orlando moved cautiously but took his little sister's hand and dragged her behind him out of the room.

Raphael didn't seem to notice, in fact it appeared to be taking all of his energy just to remain conscious.

"May as well let your son go, Raphael, we have the other six kids, their mother is dead, no way you're walking away from this mess, no need to make it any harder on yourself," Abe kept talking, making sure the man's attention was on him, and not on the fourth cop who had entered the house.

Beau moved silently, Taser in hand, and a second later Raphael collapsed with a howl of pain.

Will darted forward, grabbed Duke who had been pinned beneath his father when the man fell and pulled him away. Abe kept his gun trained on the man while Julian pulled out handcuffs and restrained him.

"You okay, Duke, any other injuries other than your face?" he asked the boy.

Ten-year-old Duke Russo looked at him with solemn brown eyes, eyes that held seriousness beyond his years and a darkness that would never completely fade away. Will knew that look. Knew that it came from seeing things you couldn't unsee, experiencing things you couldn't banish from your mind, knew that he himself had had that same look in his eyes and had seen it before in his beautiful, sweet Renee.

"I'm okay, Deputy Black," Duke replied. "I just want to see my brothers and sisters."

The kid was a fighter, Will had to give him that. He would bear scars, but he would survive, just like Renee had survived. Only now it was time for her to stop just surviving and be happy again. He prayed that he could give her that gift and repay her just once for all the times that she had saved him without her even realizing it. He prayed it wasn't too late for her, for him, or for them.

CHAPTER *Six*

August 4th
6:48 A.M.

It had been a long night, making sure the Russo kids were all checked out and then safely tucked away at their grandparents' house, getting Raphael booked, then waiting while he slept off the last of his hangover so they could interview him. Will and the others had taken turns crashing for a few hours, and now he was back at the station ready to get this case wrapped up and let River's End return to being the quaint, adorable, and safe little town that it was.

Before he focused his mind for the day, there was something he needed to do.

Will
Morning, sweetheart
Did my early Little Bird
get the worm this morning?

. . .

A smile curved his lips as he awaited her reply. He loved teasing her, and he knew without a shadow of a doubt that Renee would have been up at five, as was her custom because she had a whole, long morning routine that she went through every day. When they'd been together he had always teased her about being such an early bird.

She had always been his bird.

She soared through life, flying high above anything life threw her way. She kept her chirpy personality even when she was dealing with things that would crush most people. She sang herself to sleep each night, she rose with the birds each morning, and she chirped away to herself during the day. She was his Little Bird.

Renee
> **Rise with the sun get your day's work done**
> **Not all of us would spend half the**
> **day in bed like you, Mr. Sleepypants**

His smile grew wider. He could get used to this, starting his day talking to Renee. It would be better if he woke with her in his arms, but at least talking to her first thing in the morning was better than nothing.

> **Will**
> **If I was in bed with you right now, sweetheart**
> **The last thing we'd be doing would be sleeping**
> **;)**

Will could imagine Renee's cheeks going that cute shade of pink as she pictured all the things she knew he'd be doing if the two of them had woken side by side in their bed this morning.

. . .

Renee
You're incorrigible

Will
No, you're irresistible

Renee
Told you, you're incorrigible

As much as he didn't want to, it was time to get back to work. Raphael Russo should have sobered up by now so it was time to interview him, see if he would admit to what he'd done to Mary.

Will
Work is calling, I gotta go
Talk to you later
Love you, Little Bird

Renee
Be safe

How many times had he heard her say those words to him?
  Every time he left on a mission with his SEAL team.
  Every time he left to go undercover.
  He'd made her live in a state of constant worry. He'd been so selfish,

so wrapped up in what he wanted to do with his life that he hadn't considered her needs.

Well no more.

Never again would he put anything before Renee. She would know without a shadow of a doubt that she was number one in his life and the most precious thing he had.

Setting his phone down, Will stood and went looking for whoever else was here to do the interview with Raphael with him. Their Sheriff department was small, but they had a couple of cells usually used to house a drunk who was sleeping things off. But today, there was a murderer and kidnapper waiting for them. Once they did their interview, Raphael would be sent off to the nearest county jail where he would await trial or sentencing depending on whether he did the right thing and pled guilty or not.

He found Abe in his office on the phone.

"Yeah, sunshine, I'll be home soon, I promise, then I'll watch the little princess so you can take a break." Abe was obviously talking to his wife but waved him into the room. "Love you, too. Yeah, I can pick up more ice cream on the way. Okay, honey, see you later."

"How's baby Dawn?" he asked, leaning on the back of a chair.

"Perfection. But between the baby and the house I know Med is exhausted. She never complains though."

Pride was evident in Abe's voice and on his face, and Will couldn't help but picture Renee holding a baby in her arms. His baby. A tiny, perfect little human who was half him and half Renee. If he wanted to make that dream a reality, he knew he still had a lot of work to do, and before he could move onto phase two of his plan they needed to get this case wrapped up.

"You ready to speak to Raphael? He should have sobered up by now."

"Yeah, let's get it done so we can get off to our better halves," Abe said as he stood.

Their better halves.

That sounded pretty great.

Renee had always been his, but he'd let her down, let her forget it. He would rectify that.

Raphael was awake and pacing his cell like a caged tiger when they came to get him.

"When am I getting out of here?" he demanded when he saw them.

"You're not getting out, Raphael, not this time," Will told the man.

"You think you can keep me locked up because I took my own kids?" Raphael curled his hands around the bars and gave them an incredulous look.

"We can keep you locked up for what you did to Mary," Abe said.

The man gave a one-shouldered shrug. "So I hit her. She was going to leave, take my kids with her. I just hit her enough to knock her out so I could get the kids."

By *get* the kids the man actually meant drug the kids into unconsciousness so he could transport all seven of them without hassle. "You did a little more than just knock her out. You killed her."

At that, Raphael backed up, eyes going wide, shaking his head wildly from side to side. "Mary is dead?"

"How long did you think she could hold herself up? Days?" Will snorted.

"Hold herself up?" Raphael echoed. "What does that mean?"

He was still looking at them with a confused expression on his face. Perhaps he'd been so blind drunk when he'd done it that he had blocked it out. Or maybe Raphael would go with some sort of insanity defense and was already trying to build his case.

They knew that he had been the one to knock his wife out, the kids had told them that they'd seen their father hit their mother, then he'd given them all glasses of soda that he'd mixed sleeping pills into. By the time the kids had woken up they'd already been at the Fromyer farm. That meant there were several hours unaccounted for, plenty of time for Raphael to put up the metal bar then string his wife up on it.

If it wasn't Raphael, then who else could have killed Mary?

There was no one else in town who had any grievances with her, and according to Mary's parents, she had been ready to leave Raphael, finally realizing that he was never going to change and she and her kids deserved better. Raphael himself had just confirmed that and let them know that he'd known it. That gave him motive as well as means.

Raphael beat his wife and drank his life away. He saw his kids as a possession, *his possession*, and finding out that Mary was going to take them away from him had no doubt been the trigger that set him off. With Mary out of the picture, he could take the kids and keep them.

To top it off, Raphael had admitted to assaulting Mary and committing the kidnappings of the children. No jury in the world would believe that he hit his wife in the head to knock her out, drugged, and kidnapped his children, leaving him alone with no witnesses at the precise time that his wife was killed, but that someone else had done it.

Motive and means.

This case was a slam dunk whether Raphael was going to admit to it or not. Unless forensics of some sort turned up indicating another person had been in the house when Mary was murdered, there was no way Raphael was walking away from this.

"If you don't want to admit to it then there's no reason for you to remain here. Let's get you cuffed and transported to the county jail," Will said. There was no point in dragging it out. The quicker Raphael was locked up, the quicker Mary's parents could finalize custody of the Russo children and get them settled into their new lives with their grandparents. And the quicker this case was wrapped up, the quicker he could get to work reclaiming his woman.

11:38 A.M.

Renee blew out a breath to try to dislodge a lock of hair that had fallen loose from her ponytail. She was kneeling on the grass in the front yard of her mother's house, her hands covered in dirt as she planted seeds in the two garden beds she'd created in front of the house. The lock of hair was, of course, predictably uncooperative and she had to lift a dirt-smudged hand to brush it off her cheek and tuck it behind her ear.

It was hot out, the sky a clear sapphire blue that looked like it went on and on forever, the sun was shining brightly, and Renee made a mental note to pick up a pair of sunglasses when she ventured out next because she'd left the only pair she owned at her apartment.

Birds chirped, butterflies and the occasional dragonfly flitted about, both cats sunned themselves nearby, she was busy doing something that she loved, and yet ...

All she could think about was Will.

They had texted back and forth for a couple of hours yesterday up until he had to go to work. Given that this was a small town and small towns thrived on gossip, when she'd gone to pick up the seeds at the store early this morning, she'd heard that Mary Pino had been murdered. Everyone in River's End knew about her relationship with Raphael Russo, and knowing how he treated her, it was logical that he was the one who had killed her. Putting two and two together, she assumed that what had dragged Will off last night was arresting Raphael. With their mother dead and their father going to prison, she assumed the Russo children would be taken in by their grandparents. Mary's father was the pastor of the local church, and she knew the kids would be well taken care of, but still what a blow for the poor little things.

Shortly after her last text with Will she'd gone to bed, and ending her day talking to Will had felt so right, topped only by the fact that today had started with more messages from him.

She was falling.

And quickly.

Every time he teased her, reminded her that he still remembered every little thing about her, called her by his special pet name that no one else used, the hard shell she had covered herself with to protect her from being hurt received another little crack.

She was being weak.

She'd vowed to be strong, protect herself, and yet in just a couple of days, Will was already wearing down her shields.

Whenever she was around him, she forgot about her anger, and her pain, and all the things that she'd thought in her head over the years that she'd say to him if by chance they ever ended up in the same room.

It must be because she was lonely.

There hadn't been any men in her life since Will, and bit by bit she had distanced herself from her friends. When even the man you loved left you at your lowest point it was hard to trust that anyone else would want to be there for you.

Well, this getting close thing was stopping now.

She couldn't risk her heart again.

When it all boiled down to it, it was as simple as that.

It didn't matter that Will said he still loved her and wanted her back, and it didn't matter that she still loved him. She didn't trust him, and she wasn't putting herself in a position to let him hurt her all over again.

So no more texting.

No more letting him think there was a chance for them.

No more giving him false hope.

No more giving herself false hope.

"You look so cute—so kissable—with that dirt smudged all over your face, Little Bird."

Renee started and jerked her head up to see Will standing beside her, a bemused smile on his face and heat in his eyes as he looked down at her.

"What are you doing here?" she asked, setting the pack of seeds down as she stood, brushing her dirty hands on her denim cutoffs.

"Well, I know you're staying here for a couple of months, and I know how much you love to garden so I suspected that you might be putting in some flowerbeds and a vegetable garden while you're here. I stopped by the store this morning and spoke with someone about what I should get, they suggested celery, peppers, onions, lettuce, carrots, and beans, so voila." He held out a brown paper bag to her, and when she took it and opened it, she saw six packets of seeds inside.

"So you stopped by to drop these off?" she asked, confused about why he was trying so hard to get into her good graces when he'd had her and hadn't wanted her.

"No, I'm going to stay and help you plant them. Although I see you got a jump start," he said, indicating the areas on either side of the front door where she had removed the grass, tossed the soil, and started planting seeds.

"But you hate gardening," she reminded him. "When we were together I had to fight to get you to mow the lawn."

Regret danced across his features before he schooled them and shot her a winning smile. "But you love gardening."

"I told you before that doing all this sweet stuff isn't going to change anything, you may as well give it up." As she said the words, Renee felt a small prick of fear that he would take her at her word and do just that. It had to mean something that he was fighting for her, didn't it? The problem was, she hardly dared to hope that it would. She couldn't go back down that path with him, and yet part of her desperately needed to know that she was worth fighting for.

Will touched his thumb to his tongue and then reached out, wiping it across the dirty smudge on her cheek. "And I told you that I wasn't giving up on you."

Her mouth opened, closed, then opened again.

What did she say to that?

Did she continue to tell him to stay away, or did she accept that maybe they could learn to be friends again? After all, things couldn't really go anywhere because his life was here and she was leaving in two months.

A pang of sadness floated through her as she realized that.

"You can stay, help me garden if that's really how you want to spend your day, but only as a friend."

The smile he gave her was tender. "I'll take friendship. For now. But mark my words, Little Bird, one day I'll have all of you, heart, body, mind, and soul, and I'll never let you go. Ignore what's between us if you need to, fight against it if it makes you feel better, but nothing you do will change the outcome."

He leaned in, and Renee sucked in a breath as she waited for the feel of his lips against hers, but it never came. Instead he touched a light kiss to the tip of her nose, then winked at her.

The loss that she felt over not kissing him should have told her all she needed to know about whether she and Will were completely over or not, but she wasn't ready to go there yet. She might never be ready to go there, with him or anyone else.

"What are you planting here?" Will asked, gesturing at the two garden beds.

"Flowers," she said, trying to force her voice to come out normal and not husky as Will awakened feelings and sensations in her body that had been gone since her assault.

"What kind of flowers?"

"I wanted something that would bloom all through summer and make a spectacular array of color, so I'm planting hydrangeas, zinnias, gardenia, lavender, and crepe myrtle. By this time next summer these beds are going to be beautiful," she gushed, relaxing as she talked about her favorite hobby.

"Not as beautiful as my Little Bird." Will kissed her cheek, and a flush of warmth spread through her body. How did he make her feel so much when he did so little?

"You can help me plant these, or you can go around the back and start getting the garden ready for the vegetables you brought. If we get them planted quickly enough then depending on the weather some of them might even be producing food before I go home."

She felt rather than saw him flinch with the reminder that she wasn't here permanently, and that fact alone meant that things were never going to return to what they had been for the two of them.

To his credit, when he spoke his voice was calm and easygoing, no hint of the disappointment that she knew he felt.

Knew it because she felt it too.

"I'm here to spend time with you, so I'll stick with helping with the flowers. Maybe under your watchful eye, I'll actually get more than a muddy seed and what I plant will actually grow into the flower it's supposed to."

"You are pretty bad at gardening." She snickered, dropping back to her knees and picking up the small hand fork she'd been using. "First we need to make sure the soil is ready to go, we don't want any lumps or debris like sticks and rocks. I think even you should be able to manage that task."

"You keep up with the taunts, Little Bird, then just know I'll get you back when you least expect it," he warned with a grin on his face as he took the hand fork.

Why did that simple comment have her squirming as her lady parts tingled?

Clearing her throat, Renee continued, "We plant each seed at a depth of about three times the seed's diameter, then when they're planted we'll water them in with a nice gentle mist, nothing too hard. After that we're done, we just need to make sure they get water every day, and in no time at all the garden will be growing."

When she looked up, she saw Will watching her with a smile that made her shiver. He was serious. He really wanted her back. Knowing that made her feel so many things, happiness, anxiety, confusion, wariness, sadness. She really didn't know what she wanted. If you'd asked her a week ago she'd have told you that if Will ever came near her again, he'd be getting the brunt of the anger she'd harbored since her attack and then the cold shoulder. But old feelings didn't die down just because time had passed. She loved him, but she was too scared to give them a second chance, which left her feeling cold despite the sun's heat bearing down on her.

"Stop thinking so much, honey," Will said, reaching out to cup her face in his large hand. "Let's just plant your garden and see what grows."

Could anything grow out of the ashes of their relationship?

Renee wished she had an answer for that because if she gave him a chance and things didn't work out, then she would be the muddy seed. Too damaged to ever be any good.

～

6:13 P.M.

It had been a long day.

All Amika Chin wanted to do was get home, take off her sticky, sweaty clothes, put on a bikini, then head outside to the pool and do nothing but lounge around, sipping soda and reading, in her pool until the sun went down.

Single and still reeling from a divorce—that was anything but amicable—nearly eighteen months ago, she worked at the bank in the small town of River's End, and while the job paid well, and she liked her colleagues, she wasn't really living her dream.

This wasn't how she'd thought her life would turn out.

Thirty-two, divorced, lonely, spending her nights alone in her pool, her life was pathetic. She'd thought she'd have kids by now, but the subject of children was what had led to the breakup of her marriage in the first place. Amika had wanted kids, and her ex-husband hadn't. He'd enjoyed his life of no responsibilities. Playing golf and video games, hanging out till the early hours of the morning with his friends, partying and drinking like he was still in college and not a man in his early thirties with a job, a mortgage, and a wife. That should have been her first clue that she and Hiromi weren't on the same page when it came to the kind of life they were going to have, but she'd been in love, willing to over-look practically anything so long as she got to be a mother.

Only now she was in her thirties, single, with her biological clock ticking. It was starting to look more and more like being a mother was not in the cards for her.

Driving into her garage, Amika tried to pull herself together, she wasn't past the years of childbearing yet, and there were plenty of great single guys in River's End and the surrounding towns. If she would just stop moping and get out and meet them, maybe she would find her person.

Grabbing her purse, she got out of the car, and hit the switch on the wall to shut the garage door, then she headed inside through the interior door, into her laundry room. Pausing in there she kicked off her shoes, then stripped out of her powder blue blouse and gray pencil skirt and stuck them straight into the washing machine. Her stockings, bra, and panties followed, and then she was blessedly free of her clothing and her naked body all but cheered for joy.

Snagging her heels and purse, she headed through into the living room. She'd stick her cell phone on to charge, head upstairs to grab a bikini, and then it was time in the pool until dark when she'd heat one of the meals for one currently residing in her freezer and head to bed. A quiet, lonely evening, but at least she'd be able to relax, and maybe she could start making a plan to get her life back on the track she wanted.

Amika loved plans, charts, graphs, spreadsheets, she was definitely a geek at heart.

Just as she stepped through the laundry room door into the house's main living area, something slammed into her head.

Bright white dots immediately danced in front of her, and she staggered and fell to her knees.

What had happened?

All of a sudden it was very hard to concentrate and get her brain to focus.

Her head.

It pounded with blinding pain.

Had she walked into something?

Shoes.

Why could she see a pair of shoes in front of her?

They weren't her shoes, these were big, black boots.

Man boots.

Hiromi's?

Was he here?

She tried to get to her feet, but somehow she couldn't quite manage to get her hands beneath her and push herself up into a standing position.

Another burst of pain exploded in her head, and Amika moaned as she sank onto the cool floorboards and was dragged down into the darkness.

Pain.

Nausea.

Dizziness.

Those were the first three things that registered in her subconscious.

Amika had no idea why she felt so bad, the flu maybe, or an accident of some sort.

There was something cold around her ankle.

She had no idea what it was, and confusion was enough to get her wrenching her eyes open to find out.

When she managed to achieve the monumental task of getting her eyelids to cooperate and her vision to clear enough that she could actually see, she found herself in her kitchen. It was dark outside her windows. How long had she been here?

Slowly, fragments of memories sifted through her mind.

Being hot.

Getting home.

Stripping off.

Bikinis and her pool.

Pain in her head.

Slower than she would have liked, her brain began to fit the puzzle pieces together, and she didn't like the picture they came up with.

She hadn't slipped or fallen, someone had hit her.

At the realization, panic flooded her sense making her dizzy again.

"You have to fight against it," she ordered herself aloud, dragging in deep breath after deep breath as she tried to cling to control.

Someone had been in here with her, she'd seen shoes.

Were they still here?

Why had they knocked her out?

Had they ...

For a moment it felt like her heart actually stopped beating.

She'd been naked when she'd left the laundry room.

A glance down at her body confirmed that she was still naked.

She was naked, and there was—or had been—a stranger in her home.

Her breath quickened until it was coming so fast it wheezed in and out of her chest, and the white dots were back.

"Relax, lady, women fall at my feet and willingly offer their bodies to me, I don't have to force anyone for sex."

Her head snapped up at the sound of the voice, and she saw a man, dressed all in black, lounging in a chair at her kitchen table. He was a good-looking man, a great body, thick light brown hair, pretty greenish-blue eyes, and dimples. If he hadn't broken into her house and assaulted her, she would definitely have found him attractive.

"Wh-what are you doing here?" Amika asked, her voice shaky, fear evident in her tone.

"I'm going to kill you," he replied amicably like he hadn't just said those words.

"K-kill me?" she squeaked. Why was she so surprised to hear that? Isn't that what she'd thought he was here to do?

"It's nothing personal," he said, standing and picking up a plastic bag. "I followed a woman here, we have some unfinished business to attend to."

She had no idea what that meant or what it had to do with her. "I-I don't understand," she whimpered.

"I'm sure you don't," he said with another easy grin. "She thought she could get away by coming here, but she was wrong. I'm going to teach her a lesson she won't ever forget, and unfortunately for you, you're going to help me do that."

With that, he advanced toward her. Amika tried to back away, but she only got a foot or two when something held her in place. Her ankle. When she looked down she realized what the cold thing around her ankle had been. It was one end of metal handcuffs, the other end was secured around the pipe that ran under her sink.

"Please," she begged. "Please don't hurt me."

"No can do," he replied, kneeling in front of her. She tried to swing her free leg at him, but her movements were sluggish and uncoordinated, and he simply caught her leg and pinned it between his knees. Then he grabbed her hands and put another pair of handcuffs around her wrists.

When he picked up the bag, understanding dawned.

He was going to wrap it around her head and let her suffocate.

Panic was enough to spur her leaden limbs into movement, and she struggled as best as she could.

Of course it didn't do her any good.

He covered her face with the bag, then proceeded to knot it several times around her neck.

"See you on the other side," he told her with a pat on her head.

Through the plastic, she could make out the shape of him standing and watching her while her hands clawed at the bag. He'd put oven mitts on her hands and taped them to her wrists with duct tape.

There was no way she could rip through the plastic.

Not without her nails.

Fear choked her.

It took root in her heart, and with each beat, it flowed along with her blood throughout her body until it consumed her.

She was going to die.

Panic swelled as the plastic began to mold against her face with each desperate gasp of air she managed to drag into her lungs.

~

10:24 P.M.

Will
Work calls again, Little Bird
I'll be around tomorrow to
help with the garden beds

Renee
Stay safe
I'll see you tomorrow

Will
I love you, sweet dreams

Renee
Night

He still couldn't get an I love you out of Renee, but at least she hadn't argued with the idea of him coming back in the morning. They'd spent such a lovely day together, planting all the flowers she'd chosen and all the vegetables he'd bought. All that was left was to use some rocks to mark out the flowerbeds, and they were going to build up a small wooden fence around the vegetable garden.

They'd chatted away while they'd worked. The longer they spent together, the easier conversation became, and by the time it had started to get dark and he'd reluctantly known it was time to leave because there was only so long he could be around her and not kiss her, things had seemed like old times between them.

No sooner had Will gotten home, eaten dinner, and been ready to turn in, given that he'd been up most of the previous night he'd been ready to call it a day much earlier than usual—Renee was the early bird and he was definitely a night owl—he'd gotten a phone call.

There had been another incident.

Amika Chin, who worked at the bank in town, had been assaulted in her home. She'd been knocked out, as evidenced by the two wounds on her head, and then someone had cuffed her and tied a plastic bag around her head to suffocate her.

What was going on in River's End?

It had been such a bad year for the town, and now they'd had two violent incidents within days of each other.

His poor little town needed a break, and as much as he felt bad about it, he hoped that whoever had attacked Amika had simply taken a page out of Raphael Russo's book and decided to act out his grudge by trying to kill her.

Trying.

Because Amika Chin wasn't dead, she had survived.

"How's she doing?" he asked his cousin Levi as he stopped outside Amika's hospital room.

"Concussion, bruising, and abrasions on her ankle and wrists where she fought against the cuffs, her oxygen levels are good, she's a fighter," Levi replied. His eyes lit up as he saw something over Will's shoulder. "Hey, honey," he greeted his girlfriend as Sydney joined them.

"Hey, yourself," Sydney smiled at him. "I missed you." She stood on tiptoes to kiss Levi.

"Missed you too," he murmured against her lips as he kissed her again.

Will rolled his eyes at the lovebirds, but secretly he was jealous. He wanted Renee kissing him and telling him she missed him when they'd been apart for all of a couple of hours. "What, been like two hours since you two last saw each other?"

"More like three," Levi shot back with a grin.

Sydney giggled then turned to him. "Hey, Will. You ready to go in and interview Amika?"

"As soon as you two are done pawing at each other."

"Cousin, you need to get some and loosen up." Levi laughed.

"You're telling me," he muttered. It had been more than two years since he'd last had sex. It wasn't like he didn't get plenty of offers, but there was only one woman he wanted, and until he could have her he'd have to stick with an empty bed.

"Syd, come say bye before you leave," Levi told his girlfriend as he gave her one last kiss.

"Maggie and Poppy told me about Renee, I hope things work out for you two," Sydney told him as Levi walked away and they headed for Amika's room.

"I do too," he agreed as he opened the door.

Inside the room, Amika Chin lay in the bed. The lights were on but dimmed, the room was warm but Amika had several blankets on, pulled up to her chin. Her eyes were closed, dark brown hair fanned out on the pillows around her face, her head was bandaged, and she looked like she was sleeping.

As soon as she heard them though her eyes popped open. "Will, Sydney," she said softly.

"Hey, Am, how you feeling?" he asked as he crossed to the bed and pulled up the single chair in the room, indicating to Sydney that she should take it.

"Like there's a riot in my brain," Amika replied.

"I know the feeling," he grimaced. He'd suffered plenty of concussions over the years, from playing football in high school to being a SEAL, to working undercover.

"Mind if we ask you a few questions? We'll keep it brief," Sydney promised.

"It's okay. I want you to find this guy before he hurts someone else," Amika told them.

"Why would you think he's going to hurt someone else?" he asked, it sounded like this might not have been personal.

"Just from some of the things he said." Amika shrugged but then winced at the movement.

"Do you know him?" he asked.

"No, and I've never seen him before."

"Do you think you could work with a sketch artist? Give us a description of him?" he asked.

"I got a good look at his face, he wasn't hiding it, so I think I should be able to give a good description," Amika informed them.

"Why don't you tell us what you remember, starting at the beginning," Sydney suggested.

"Okay." Amika pulled her hands out from underneath the blanket and began to fidget with the hem. "I got home from work, and I was hot because the air conditioning at the bank has been down the last few days, so I stripped as soon as I got home, dumped my stuff in the washer, and was going to get my bikini on to spend the night in the pool.

He knew from the dispatcher that when Amika had gone running out of her house to her neighbors, she'd been naked. There was no way his mind could not go back to that night he had arrived home to find Renee naked and tied to their bed. He still regularly had nightmares about it. Of all the things he'd seen and done in his life that was the single worst.

"Am, I hate to ask, but did he sexually assault you?" he asked softly.

Her cheeks turned bright pink, but she shook her head. "I don't think so, not while I was awake at least, and he said that he wasn't there to do that because he could get any woman he wanted."

Relief swamped him that she'd been spared. Most days, Will had no idea how Renee found the strength to go on after she'd been through something so horrific. But she had, and that only made him love her more.

"What happened after you put your things in the washing machine?" Sydney asked.

"I went through to the living room, and pain exploded in my head. I remember being dazed and trying to get up and then more pain in my head. I must have passed out, been out for a while because it was dark when I woke up. I panicked at first and then I saw the man. He told me that he was going to kill me, that it was nothing personal, and that there was a chance I could get free. Then he put the cuffs on my wrist, my ankle was already cuffed to a pipe under the sink, and he tied the bag on. I tried to get it off, must have passed out briefly, then I somehow managed to claw it free. After that, I broke the pipe apart and ran." Amika finished her tale and reached up to brush at her wet eyes.

"You were amazing to get yourself free like that," he assured her, reaching out to grasp one of her hands and squeeze.

"Thanks," she whispered.

"Did he say anything else to you?" Sydney asked.

"He said that he was here because he had unfinished business with someone and that he was going to use me to teach her a lesson. He said that he had just followed the woman here to River's End."

Will froze.

The killer had just followed a woman to River's End.

Renee had just moved back to River's End.

A flashback from a few days ago when he'd found her at the grocery store came to mind. She'd told him she was back in town to housesit because she had needed a break. When she'd said that he'd gotten the feeling that there was more to it than she was saying.

Was Renee the woman the killer was talking about?

Was she in some sort of trouble?

If she was, why hadn't she told him?

She had to know that even if things weren't great between them that there wasn't anything he wouldn't do to make sure she was safe.

And right now, his gut told him that she was anything but safe.

CHAPTER
Seven

August 5th
7:09 A.M.

A glance at her phone showed that there were no messages she had missed.

Just like the last dozen times she'd checked it.

Each time Renee made sure that she hadn't accidentally set it on silent, then checked that she still had reception and the phone was charged.

She was being ridiculous.

She knew that.

Why was it all of a sudden such a big deal that she hadn't heard from Will since he said goodnight last night?

For two years he hadn't texted her first thing in the morning, in fact the only day that he had was yesterday morning, so this was hardly anything out of the ordinary. And even before they'd broken up, she was used to going days, weeks, or sometimes even months without contact from him.

So why was today so different?

She'd been up since five, done some yoga, taken a shower, tried to eat breakfast but found that her stomach was too churned up and she couldn't get anything down. Then she'd watered the garden and made sure they had everything they'd need for later when Will came to help her finish off the garden beds.

Now she was just sitting.

Waiting.

For Will to text.

This was such a mistake. She was already in way too deep, deep enough that she didn't know how she would walk away when her mom came home, and she went back to her life. Deep enough that she knew she would never be completely free of Will Black. He was imprinted on her soul too deeply, he was tattooed on her heart, he was connected to her in ways she didn't even understand.

Even though she knew better, she reached out and checked her phone again, and once again, there were no messages sitting there that she had missed. Had he been hurt last night on whatever work-related thing he'd headed out on?

Worry and anxiety churned in her gut.

What if something had happened to him? What if he wasn't okay? What if he was hurt? Worse, what if he was dead?

Renee knew that she wasn't a part of Will's life anymore, and yet the thought of him not being around felt like someone had sliced her heart in half.

The doorbell rang, and she just about jumped off the chair she'd been sitting in, pretending to be doing a little work, and darted for the door. Was this someone with bad news? Was Will really dead? She was sure that if he was gone she would know it, she would feel it. Wouldn't she?

With hands that were shaking much more than they should over a man who had broken her heart and all but destroyed her, she flung open the door and immediately let out a breath of relief.

Something flared in Will's eyes at her exhale, and he quirked up one side of his mouth in a half-smile. "You worried about me, Little Bird?"

She didn't know what to say to that. If she said no, she'd be lying, but if she told him the truth and said yes, she'd be further encouraging his hope that the two of them would get back together.

Before she had to make a decision on what she would say, she realized that he wasn't alone on her doorstep. There was a tall man with brown hair she'd never seen before there as well.

Somehow, she didn't think this was a social call.

For some reason that spiked her anxiety, and when she looked back at Will and saw the guilt he tried to hide in his eyes that anxiety jumped through the roof.

Why was he feeling guilty?

"This is Beau," Will said.

"Poppy's boyfriend." She nodded. "You joined the Sheriff's department."

"Nice to meet you, Ms. Miller," Beau said.

They were here on police business.

Her mind immediately went to the reason she'd been so eager to come and housesit for her mom. There was no way they could know about that, and even if they did, they couldn't arrest her for it. She hadn't known until it was too late, if she had she would have done things differently, but she was a lawyer, and she knew she hadn't done anything illegal.

So why did she feel like she deserved to be handcuffed and thrown in a cell?

"What's going on?" she asked, shaking away her fears.

"We need to talk to you," Will said. His voice was deliberately gentle but it did nothing to ease her worries.

"Did I do something wrong?"

"No, of course not, we just need to talk," Will assured her.

"Is my mom okay? My dad? My sister and brothers?" None of her family were in River's End, but she knew that if something had happened Will would make sure he was the one to break the news.

"Renee, look at me." Will stepped closer, took both her hands in his, and looked steadily at her until she met his gaze. "No one is hurt, you're not in trouble, and nothing is wrong. We just want to ask you a couple of questions about something that happened last night and what the victim told us. All right?"

Since he looked so sincere, she nodded. "All right."

Keeping hold of her hand, Will led her inside, guided her into a seat on the couch, and then sat beside her, her hand still in his. Beau had followed them in, closed the front door, and took a seat in the armchair opposite the couch. They exchanged a look that obviously was some sort of code because Beau leaned forward a little and started talking.

"Last night a woman was attacked in her home. The man tried to kill her by tying a plastic bag over her head, in her panicked thrashing the bag broke and she was able to escape. She said that before he put the bag on her head, he told her that he was here because he wanted to teach someone else a lesson, and killing her would do that. He also told her that he had just followed a woman here, that she was the one he was trying to teach a lesson."

What was she supposed to say to that?

It was clear they thought that she was this woman, but why? Surely she wasn't the only woman who had recently arrived in town.

"You think she's talking about me?"

"Could she be?" Beau asked.

"I don't see why she would be. It's summer, there are plenty of tourists around, and I'm sure lots arrived within the last few days. I don't think this has anything to do with me."

"Are you sure?" Will asked. "Have any of the people you defended recently threatened you? Any families angry that you didn't get their loved one off or a lighter sentence?"

"I get threats on a daily basis, it's part of the job," she said and didn't miss his flinch. "But you know I mostly work with people who didn't get a fair trial for some reason or another and who I believe are innocent."

"Your boss makes you take other cases sometimes too though," Will prodded.

"Yeah, sometimes," she replied, thinking of the last time she worked one of those cases. She'd believed that the man had been innocent, what an idiot she'd been. There was no way she was telling them about that, she was way too embarrassed about her chronic lack of judgment.

"Renee, is there anyone who might have a grudge against you who would have followed you here, who wants to hurt you?" Beau asked.

"There's no one," she answered firmly and was ninety-nine percent sure that she was correct.

"Our victim is going to be working with a sketch artist today. Can we bring the sketch around once we have it, see if it reminds you of anyone?" Beau asked.

"I guess," she answered even though she didn't want to. She wanted no part of this case, but on the slim chance she did happen to know the man who had tried to kill someone then she'd take a look at the picture. It couldn't hurt.

Unlike this game she and Will were playing.

Seeing him like this again when he wasn't being all charming and trying to woo her just reminded her of why their relationship had fallen apart in the first place.

His job would always come first.

"Beau, I'll meet you in the car," Will said. Once they were alone, he lifted the hand he still held and kissed it. "I'm going to be tied up with this case today, but I'll stop by when I can, okay?"

Maybe it wasn't fair to be upset that once again his job was coming before her, but she couldn't help it. She'd allowed his games to work, she'd allowed herself to get sucked back in, and now she was realizing that nothing had really changed.

Tugging her hand free, she stood because she needed some space so that she could think clearly. "I don't think you should come back, Will. This *thing* we're doing is only going to end in more pain. I'm leaving in a couple of months, and your job is here." She didn't bother to mention that they both knew his job would always come before her. It was what it was, and he had dedicated his entire adult life to keeping others safe so she could hardly fault him for taking his job so seriously.

"There are so many ways we can work around that," Will said.

She just shook her head. Nothing had changed on his end so nothing could change things on her end. "I think it's best that we keep our distance while I'm here."

Because she knew she would burst into tears at any second, she turned and hurried upstairs, leaving Will to let himself out. This felt like losing him all over again. Letting go was just as hard, but there was no way she could take the risk of letting him all the way back in, knowing that sooner or later, he would let her down again.

～

5:40 P.M.

For a day when all she had done was lie on a towel in her swimsuit at the side of her pool, Renee felt surprisingly stressed. The warm sun on her skin, the blue sky, the gentle breeze, the buzzing bees and fluttering butterflies, the soft grass beneath her, none of it could do a single thing to help her relax.

She didn't want to do anything. Not go down to the river to swim, not garden, not read or watch TV, not even eat. All she was doing was just lying here staring aimlessly into space and trying to get her head on straight.

It was all Will's fault.

She was second-guessing herself and her decision to cut him out.

He was trying really hard, he'd apologized several times for leaving her the way he had, and he'd admitted that he made a mistake, and he'd been making such an effort to be sweet and kind and do nice things for her. She knew that he hated gardening and yet he'd spent a large portion of the day yesterday planting flower and vegetable seeds. Today notwithstanding, he'd texted her throughout the day even though he had been at work. Will had been honest with her about wanting her back and told her several times that he loved her and that he wasn't giving up on her.

Maybe she should be making the same effort as he was.

After all, she did still love him.

After everything that she had been through, did she really want to let him go when he wanted her back?

Isn't this the one thing she wanted more than anything else; to finally put the past behind her and move on with her life?

Why was it so hard?

Trusting him again, letting him into her heart again, giving him the ability to hurt her again, made her want to run and hide and never see Will again because it was just easier.

But nothing worth having was easy.

That's what she'd always believed, and from her experience that was the way it was. When she was thirteen, she'd taken a bad fall off her horse, broken her back, for a while she had been confined to a wheelchair. Being stuck in bed for months at a time, unable to get out and do things with her friends had taught her patience. Learning to walk again, going through hours of grueling physical therapy had taught her determination. Dealing with pain every single day for well over a year had taught her strength.

Patience, determination, and strength sounded like a recipe for a successful life, yet all of those skills seemed to have fled the second she was tied to that bed, and her body was violated.

She wanted her old self back.

She wanted her strength back.

Maybe if she could find the person she used to be, she and Will would have a chance.

Yet she couldn't get over the idea that Will had left her, hurt her, abandoned her, if she took him back she was sure that made her a fool.

"Argh," she groaned aloud, rubbing at her temples. "I'm so sick of thinking about this. I don't want to be stuck in my head anymore, I just want to move on. I want to *move on.*"

How desperately she wished that she knew what to do.

Annoyed with herself she got up, left her towel behind, and stalked into the house.

She would find a way to stop waffling about what she wanted and figure it out. Either she could forgive Will for hurting her and find a way to move forward, or she couldn't, and if she couldn't then she had to remain firm and keep her distance from him because anything else wasn't fair.

Movement caught her attention as she stepped inside but the brightness of the outdoors contrasted with the dullness of indoors meant it took a moment for her vision to settle enough to see what was happening, and by then it was too late.

Something slammed into her head, and the world around her ceased to exist.

Minutes might have passed.

Hours maybe.

Renee had no idea when she finally started to emerge from the darkness.

Something had made her wake up.

What was it?

Water.

She was wet.

Was it raining?

She'd been out by the pool, maybe she'd fallen asleep.

Water closed over her head, and it snapped her out of her daze.

"Better swim if you don't want to die," a voice whispered in her ear.

This wasn't just rain, there was too much water, and it was everywhere, all over her.

Her arms and legs flailed as her eyes opened to find herself in the pool.

How had she gotten in here?

Maybe she had fallen asleep and been dreaming. It wasn't unheard of for her to dream so vividly about the night of her assault that she would wake, drenched in sweat, on the floor, battling a villain that was no longer there.

Was that what had happened?

No, if that was true, why had she heard someone talking?

Something was *really* wrong with her because she couldn't seem to figure anything out.

When her brain finally communicated with her body that she needed to do something to get out of the pool, she began to splash with her arms, but she was cold and her body felt funny, off somehow. Renee tried to swim back to the edge of the large pool, but something was stopping her. Something was weighing her down, trying to drag her under the water. What was going on?

Scared, cold, and hurting, she choked back a sob.

Her neck.

There was something around her neck.

Shaking hands moved to touch it as she kicked with her legs.

Rope.

There was rope around her neck.

The rope went off down toward the bottom of the pool. There was tension on it so it wasn't just floating down there, it had to be tied to something.

What was going on?

How did she get in the pool with a killer headache and a rope around her neck tied to something that was preventing her from swimming to the edge of the pool? And who had told her to swim if she didn't want to die?

Her breathing was quickening, and she used every ounce of strength she had to try to get to the edge of the pool. She wanted out of the water. Now. But she couldn't seem to swim more than a yard or so in any one direction. Whatever the rope was tied to was heavy and obviously designed to keep her stuck out here, unable to get to the edge.

She was going to die.

That knowledge hit her like a sledgehammer.

It was dark out, and she lived alone. She'd told Will that she thought they shouldn't spend any more time around each other and there were only so many times she could tell him that before he believed her and honored her wishes and stayed away. Even if he did decide to come back it was clearly nighttime, he'd be home by now, and at best wouldn't come until tomorrow morning.

Hours away.

There was no way she could survive that long.

Already her body was tiring, and her head hurt so bad.

That must have been how he got her in the pool and attached to this rope, he must have knocked her unconscious and then done this to her.

Her mind immediately snapped to the attack that Will and Beau had told her about. Was this the same person? Had he really followed her here to River's End?

A moving figure caught her attention.

"Help," she called out, worried about how weak her voice sounded.

The figure said nothing just moved closer to the pool and stood there, and she understood.

It was the man who had done this to her.

She could ask him why he'd done it, who he was, what he wanted from her, but it wasn't worth the energy. He wouldn't answer, and she had to conserve as much strength as she could because she had to keep treading water until someone found her. The rope around her neck only allowed her to just keep her head above the water, but when exhaustion took over she would sink.

Drown.

She was going to die here, in this pool, alone.

Just like she'd been alone when she'd fallen off that horse out in the forest, forced to drag herself on her stomach, enduring excruciating pain, until she got back close enough to the stables for someone to find her.

Just like she'd been alone when that man had broken into her home, tied her up, and raped her, ripping away pieces of herself she was still trying to find two years later.

Now she was alone, and this time she would drown.

As her body shook with cold and her arms and legs desperately worked to keep her head above water, Renee realized that maybe she had already forgiven Will, but fear and distrust had held her back. At least she'd had a nice couple of days with him before she died.

CHAPTER
Eight

August 6th
6:56 A.M.

Will
Little Bird, I'm worried about you
Please reply even if its
just to tell me to go away

Just like every other text he'd sent since he and Beau had gone to ask her if she could be the woman that this would-be killer was supposedly following, despite her asking him to stay away he just couldn't do that. He hated that she was hurting, that she'd run away in tears to hide from him, but maybe this was what she needed, to finally confront everything that had happened instead of trying to ignore it.

This was what they both needed.

He needed her like he needed his next breath of air and he'd meant what he said when he'd told her that he wasn't walking away.

Renee needed him, he was sure of it. She was coping with what had happened the best way she could, but she had unresolved issues about it, one of which was his reaction and response. If they could just get past that, clear the air, then he was sure that they could get back what he'd ruined. He wished she'd just unleash her pent-up anger and pain on him instead of trying to hold it in.

But before he could convince her to do that, he had to make sure she was safe.

She was hiding something from him.

There was more to her story than she'd said, she was here because she was running from something—or someone.

By the time he parked his car outside Renee's house he still hadn't heard anything from her.

> **Will**
> **I'm here at your house**
> **I'm not leaving till we talk**
> **So you can let me in or I**
> **can break down the door**
> **I love you, Little Bird,**
> **and I'm not letting you**
> **slip away, we need to talk,**
> **clear the air, so we can**
> **move forward**
> **Together in case that wasn't clear**

Again there was no answer, and he couldn't help but be concerned. He had that bad feeling in his gut again, the same feeling he'd had the night he'd found her tied to the bed.

Something was wrong.

Gun in hand, he jumped out of his car and ran to the front door, hammering on it. "Renee, are you in there?" he yelled. "I need to see you. I'm worried about you."

There was no response, and he couldn't hear any sounds of someone moving around in there.

Circling the house, intending to check the back door, when he got into the backyard he could hear splashing.

Relief nearly knocked him over.

Renee was just out in the pool swimming, that was why she hadn't replied to his texts this morning.

Putting his gun away, he strolled toward the pool, a smile on his face, ready to tell Renee that he'd cook her breakfast and then the two of them were going to talk, really talk.

That smile faded when he got closer to the pool.

Renee wasn't in there swimming laps, she was floundering, splashing about, her head going under then bobbing back above the surface only to disappear again.

With no idea what was going on, Will dropped his weapon, phone, and wallet on the ground and dived into the water, his eyes immediately zeroing in on what looked like a rope. He came up beside Renee, pulling her up against his body, his arm wrapped across her chest, holding her head above the water.

She coughed and spluttered, choking on the water she'd no doubt been swallowing. "Renee, what's going on?" he demanded

"Rope ... neck ... can't move ... cold ... tired ..." she mumbled incoherently. Her body trembled in his hold and her teeth chattered as she tried to talk. How long had she been in here?

"Okay, sweetheart, I got you now." A million questions ran through his head, but now wasn't the time to worry about them. The rope around her neck had to be tied to something heavy to prevent Renee from getting out of the water. "Let me look at this rope so I can get you out of here." Keeping her pressed against his chest with one arm, he used his other to try and pry at the rope, get it undone. He cursed under his breath when he couldn't get the thin strands to budge. "Hold on, Renee, I'm going to swim down and see if I can untie the other end."

Reluctantly letting go of her, Will dived down, following the rope to find it was tied to a rock. This was like a scene out of a bad mob movie, bodies weighed down with rocks, only this perverse killer had thrown her in here alive to let her die slowly, forcing her to wait until exhaustion claimed her limbs and she could no longer keep her head above water.

His fingers fumbled with the rope, but whoever had tied it had done a good job, he didn't think he could undo it, at least not quickly enough.

Lungs screaming, Will went back to the surface to drag in a breath of air.

"Will?" Renee said, he could see her struggling, fighting but coming closer to failing keeping herself afloat.

"I can't untie it, I'll try to pick it up, move it closer to the edge so you can get out."

Giving her a quick kiss on the forehead, he swum back down. At the bottom of the pool he tried to lift the rock but it was huge and he couldn't seem to get it to budge. He pushed it, then tried to use the rope to pull it, yanking on it until the rope burned the palms of his hands.

Above him he could see that Renee's struggles were getting weaker, and he quickly swum back up, taking her in his arms again.

"Baby, I'm going to have to leave you for a moment, go inside and get a knife to cut through this."

"Don't leave me," she panicked, thrashing in his grip as she clutched desperately at him.

"It's only for a moment, baby. I'll be right back, you just have to keep your head above water for me."

"I can't," she sobbed.

They were wasting precious energy she didn't have debating it. Ripping out his heart in the process he let go of her and swam back to the edge of the pool. "You can do this, Little Bird."

Her terrified sobs echoed behind him as he hoisted himself out of the water and ran across the yard. The back door was wide open, and he ran inside, purposefully ignoring the blood on the floor as he grabbed a knife from the block on the counter.

By the time he made it back to the pool, Renee had gone under.

Heart in his throat, he jumped in, swam straight toward where he could see her floating, and broke the surface with her in his arms.

"Hold on, baby." Again he had to balance her now limp body

against his chest while he trod water to keep them both above the surface while he cut through the rope, careful not to pierce her flesh.

As soon as he got her free, he let the rope and the knife go and swam them to the steps. He had to get her out of the water as quickly as possible. She was already too cold.

Shifting her so she was cradled in his arms, he ran up the couple of steps out of the pool then laid her down on the tiles. She wasn't moving, her eyes were closed, and he pressed his fingers to her neck, his cheek above her mouth as he checked to see if she was breathing. He felt a pulse but couldn't feel a puff of air against his skin.

Tilting her head back, he pinched her nose closed, covered her mouth with his, and breathed into her.

"Come on, Little Bird, don't you dare leave me. I want a chance to prove to you that I'm never going to let you down again, I want a chance to get you back," he pleaded with her.

She didn't stir, and he breathed into her again, begging God not to take her from him.

Then he heard the most beautiful sound ever.

Renee coughed and spluttered, coughing up water.

He rolled her onto her side so the water could come out. "There you go, baby, you're doing great."

"Will?" she croaked.

"Right here," he assured her as he eased her onto her back and smoothed her wet hair off her face.

"You came back," she wheezed.

While he hated that she had doubted him, he hoped this proved to her that he was all in, he was never leaving her again. "I'll always come back for you, my Little Bird."

She nodded, her tired eyes falling closed, her entire body shaking violently. If she'd been in the water all night, battling to stay afloat, then she was probably hypothermic, or borderline hypothermic, he had to warm her up. Spotting a towel on the ground by the pool, he snagged it and wrapped it around Renee, then shed his wet jeans and t-shirt so he could use his body heat to help warm her.

Grabbing his phone and gun, he picked Renee up and carried her inside where he sat on the couch, settled her on his lap, then tucked the towel around both of them. Once he had her settled, he called for an ambulance and cops to come and secure the scene.

"It's all right now, sweetheart," he crooned, cradling her head in his hand and kissing her forehead.

"You saved me," she said softly. "Thank you."

"That is something you never have to thank me for," he told her, dragging her closer. "Don't you know by now that you're a part of me? Renee, I love you, I always loved you, and I always will love you. You're mine. It's as simple as that. You belong to me just like I belong to you. I would move mountains for you, I would go into the depths of Hell for you, I would die for you. You're my little bird, and I love you more than anything, more than life itself."

~

7:29 A.M.

She couldn't get warm.

She was snuggled on Will's lap, pressed up against his bare skin, the towel tucked around her, but she couldn't stop shaking.

Renee had been convinced that she would die in that pool.

The hours had bled one into another as she'd stared at the inky black sky with the thousands of twinkling diamonds, blinking and winking at her, while she tried desperately to keep treading water while also trying not to pass out as the pain in her head intensified.

Then Will had been there, holding her up in his strong arms, keeping her head above the water, taking her weight so she didn't have to swim any longer.

If he hadn't found her, she'd be dead.

"My head hurts," she whimpered as she pressed herself closer.

"I know it does, baby." Will's lips were on the top of her head, his arms like steel bands wrapped around her, keeping her cocooned in a little bubble of safety. "Ambulance is on the way. When the medics get here, they'll give you something for the pain."

"So tired." Her eyes wanted so badly to close, but she was afraid that if she went to sleep when she woke up again Will rescuing her would all have been a dream, and she'd be back in the pool, fighting to stay alive.

"Try to stay with me, sweetheart," Will pleaded, fear evident in his voice. "I know you're tired, and when the medics get here then you can rest, but for now, just stay with me. Please, baby."

For Will she would try.

For the next few minutes she laid against him, trying to stay awake, letting the feel of Will's arms wrapped around her calm her.

Sirens sounded, and a minute later there was a knock at the door. Will stood with her in his arms and carried her to the door.

Paramedics entered, and she was poked and prodded, given something to ease the headache, wrapped in so many blankets she felt like a swaddled baby, and bundled into the ambulance. Finally free from pain and slowly starting to warm up, Renee felt herself slipping away. She wanted to ask Will to stay with her, but exhaustion had wrapped its tentacles around her and was pulling her under.

When she woke up next, she was finally warm.

It was so wonderful that she couldn't help but give a delighted moan.

"Renee?"

Gentle pressure on her hand told her that even though she hadn't had a chance to ask, Will had stayed by her side anyway.

"Sweetheart, can you hear me?"

As much as she wanted to stay in her little bubble of warmth and sleepiness, she knew that Will would be worried about her. "I can hear you."

"You scared me." She could hear the relief in his voice, and his fingers began to caress her face. "Can you open your eyes for me?"

He didn't know what a monumental task he was asking of her, but for Will, she would try. When she managed to do as he'd asked, she saw his anxious face looking down at her. The smile that transformed his face when he saw her awake and looking at him warmed her more than all the blankets in the world could have.

"How're you feeling?"

"Better. My head doesn't hurt so badly, and I feel warmer. I'm just tired."

"They're going to keep you here for a few hours so you'll be able to get plenty of rest."

She opened her mouth to ask if he'd be staying, but there was a knock on the door, and a moment later it opened and Will's cousins Abe and Levi walked in. She hadn't seen either since she'd been back in town, but both looked just the way she remembered them, only Abe actually looked relaxed.

"How's my favorite patient?" Levi grinned at her as he walked over to the opposite side of the bed to where Will was standing and picked up her wrist to take her pulse.

"I'm feeling better."

"That makes me happy to hear. Your vitals are all stable, and your temperature is back up. You've got a concussion so we'll be keeping you here for the rest of the day to monitor you. Assuming everything looks good then you can go home around dinnertime. Sound good?"

"Yeah," she answered a little hesitantly. She was nervous to go back to the house where she had almost died and stay there alone for the next two months until her mom returned home.

"If you don't want to go back there then Maggie already said she'd set you up in a room at the hotel," Will told her, reading her mind.

That was good to know, but she'd wait to make her decisions until it was time for her to be discharged.

"She up to an interview, Levi?" Abe asked his brother.

"Renee?" Levi handballed the question onto her.

She wanted to say no because she didn't even want to think about what had happened to her, but she knew she couldn't do that. "Yeah, I guess."

"Physically, she's up to it, but emotionally if she becomes upset I'm putting a stop to it," Levi told his brother.

"Fair enough." Abe cracked a smile, his whole face transformed when he did. She'd known the Black boys pretty much all their lives, and she didn't think she'd ever seen Abe so relaxed and happy. She was glad he'd found someone who gave him that peace he needed, and Meadow seemed nice.

Will perched on the edge of her bed, still holding one of her hands,

Levi remained protectively on her other side, and Abe pulled up the room's other chair.

"Can you tell us what you remember?" Abe asked her.

Nodding nervously, her fingers tightened around Will's. "I was lying out by the pool and was ready to go inside. I remember walking through the back door and then nothing." Her free hand moved absently to touch the spot on the side of her head that was pulsing even though it didn't really hurt. Levi caught her fingers and gently pulled them away from the wound setting her hand back down on the mattress.

"What do you remember next?" Abe asked with a gentleness that belied the big, gruff man.

"I felt water and was confused, someone told me to swim if I didn't want to die. It took me a while to figure out that I was in the pool and a rope was tied around my neck. It must have been tied to something heavy because it wouldn't let me pull it to the edge of the pool. I was stuck. My head hurt, I was dizzy and cold, and so tired, but I kept swimming."

"Yeah, you did," Will said proudly, leaning over to kiss her cheek.

His pride warmed her a little more. "I saw a man, but not enough to see what he looked like, it was dark out. I kept swimming for what felt like hours, I was so tired. It was getting harder and harder to keep my head above water, and then Will was there."

She looked over at him and saw his eyes were bright with unshed tears. She could feel his fear, he knew how close he'd come to losing her, and she could see how badly that scared him.

"Yesterday, when Beau and I asked, you said you didn't think anyone might have followed you here to get back at you. Do you still think that?" Will asked her.

As much as she really didn't want to tell anyone about the horrible mistake that she had made, if it was him and he was here in River's End, he'd already tried to kill her and an innocent person. She might deserve it, but no one else did.

"Do you know something, Renee?" Abe asked.

"I don't know," she said softly. What would Will think of her when he knew how awfully she had messed up? He had given his whole life to saving others, and while he'd never held it against her that she was a defense attorney, she knew that sometimes he'd wished that she would change jobs to work for the DA. As much as she would enjoy fighting for justice for victims, she was doing that too. So many people had been falsely convicted, and she loved that she was able to help them get their own justice.

"Why don't you tell us and we'll see if we think it's something we need to look into," Abe coaxed.

Because she knew she didn't really have a choice, if it was him and she didn't say anything, and he killed someone because of her she'd never be able to live with it. "It was someone I represented. He was charged with multiple counts of rape and murder. The cops thought he had been breaking into homes of women who lived alone, raping them, and then drowning them. He claimed that he was innocent, and yes, I know most criminals say that, but he had compelling evidence."

"What was it?" Abe asked.

"Surveillance footage of him at a woman's apartment and her statement that she was with him on the nights that two of the five murders occurred. I believed that he was innocent, and when I presented the case, twelve jurors agreed with me. He was found not guilty on all charges."

"But he was guilty?"

"The day after the trial he came to my office, I thought it was just to say thank you for everything, but it wasn't. He told me that he did it, that he paid the woman to testify, and that he paid someone to doctor that footage. Double jeopardy, he couldn't be charged with the murders again. I knew he would keep raping and killing and I told him that when he got caught again I would make sure he spent the rest of his life in prison. I really believed him, he fooled me, I fell for it all," she finished quietly, burning with shame for the mistake she had made and the people who would be hurt because of it.

"Hey," Will said with such force that she shrunk away from him. "Are you beating yourself up about this?" At her minuscule nod, he continued, "He tricked you. He had evidence that you had no reason to doubt, and you have the biggest, purest heart in the world. You want to believe the good in everyone, it's one of the things that I love the most about you." He grabbed her face and pulled her in for a fierce kiss before releasing her.

"You can't take the blame for that, Renee," Abe agreed. "That's all on him. What's his name?"

"You've probably heard of the family. It was Josiah Holdsworthy III. His family owns a huge real estate development company, they're worth billions. Josiah is a trust fund baby; he doesn't work, just parties and sleeps around. He acts like he's nineteen and not twenty-nine. His attitude to life and sense of entitlement should have clued me in, but he had this huge sob story about how his family treated him badly and wouldn't let him do what he really wanted to in life, and I fell for it," she finished on a sigh.

"Baby, please stop trying to take responsibility for his actions. He didn't just trick you, he fooled twelve of his peers as well," Will reminded her.

"I guess," she said, then yawned so big she felt her jaw click. Her eyes were getting heavy, and it was getting harder to concentrate.

Noticing that, Levi immediately reached over to fiddle with her IV, injecting something into it. "That's all for now, guys, she needs to rest. Renee, I've given you some more painkillers and something to help you sleep."

"Okay." She yawned again. Whatever he gave her was obviously starting to work.

"Get some rest. We'll get this guy, okay? Whether it's Josiah or someone else," Abe promised.

"I don't know why he'd come after me," she said, fighting to keep her eyes open.

"It's not your job to figure it out," Will said, kissing the tip of her nose. "Just rest, rebuild your strength, and let us take care of it."

Right.

Of course, Will would be leaving her now to work this case.

Why had she thought anything would be different this time?

He hadn't been there for her when she'd been raped, and now he was getting ready to leave her all over again.

She really was stupid.

And a slow learner.

As the drugs claimed her a single tear rolled down her cheek and then she drifted away.

~

"Little Bird, ready to be sprung?" Will asked with a grin as he walked back into her hospital room. Over the last several hours, Renee had mostly slept, replenishing the energy she'd spent trying to keep herself alive last night. Her vitals had remained stable, she said the pain in her head had subsided, and for the last hour she had been all but climbing the walls ready to escape.

"More than ready," she said, springing off the bed, then wincing. She quickly brushed it off in her excitement and pulled on the jacket that Meadow had dropped off earlier. Renee had been wearing nothing but a skimpy bathing suit when she'd been attacked, and he hadn't wanted her to have to go home in scrubs so he'd sent a quick message to his cousin's wife and asked her to drop by Renee's and pick up some clothes.

"Let's get you out of here." He slung an arm around her shoulders and led her through the hospital. He'd left his car close to the door, and once he'd helped her inside and climbed into the driver's seat, he asked, "Where do you want to go? Back to your mom's or the hotel?" He'd prefer to take her to his place where he knew she'd feel safe and where he could keep an eye on her, but he knew that she wasn't in that place yet. She still had to get used to the idea of them as a couple again.

"Umm," she hesitated, clearly struggling to make a decision.

"Whatever you choose is fine, there's no right or wrong," he told her as he started the engine. He didn't want to mention yet that if she decided to go back to her mom's he'd be staying there with her tonight. She had a concussion, and she'd nearly drowned, not to mention the fact that she'd been traumatized. There was no way she would be alone right now.

"I should probably go back to my mom's, no point in putting it off, I can't put it off forever. Besides, I need to look after the cats."

"But you *can* put it off for as long as you need to. And the cats can come with you to my place."

"You don't like cats."

"I like them enough to help you take care of them until your mom comes back."

"Thank you, but I'd rather just get it over and done with. Like pulling off a Band-Aid."

"Like pulling off a Band-Aid," he agreed, but he had a bad feeling about this. It wasn't that he thought the man who'd attacked her would come back, but Renee was trying to take her emotions and shove them into a box rather than dealing with them. That was a recipe for disaster. There was only so long you could do that before they came exploding out, and he had to wonder how close Renee was to exploding.

The ride to her house was quiet, but that kind of comfortable quiet between people who knew each other well, and didn't feel the need to fill every second with idle chitchat.

By the time he was pulling into the driveway, Renee looked about ready to crash again. Levi had said not to worry about the lack of energy, that it would just take time for her body to recover, particularly as it dealt with the concussion coupled with the trauma. Once he got her inside, he'd make her some dinner and then she could go off to bed.

"Wait while I come around to open your door and help you out," he said, undoing his seatbelt.

"Were you this bossy when we were together?" she asked, but there was a smile in her voice.

"Pretty sure I was worse," he said with a laugh.

She waited for him to come around, open her door for her, and didn't resist when he wrapped an arm around her waist to support her as he walked her to the front door. Inside, he led her to the couch and eased her down on to it. Reaching for a pillow and fluffing it up, he set it behind her, then grabbed a throw that was folded over the back of a chair and spread it over her.

"What?" he asked when he saw her giving him a bemused smile.

"I forgot how much you fuss like a mother hen. Remember the time

I had my appendix out? You fussed about me for two straight weeks afterward, would hardly leave my side." Her smile became a fond one as she reminisced.

"I remember. And if I recall things correctly, someone loved all my fussing, my homemade soups, my sponge baths, and being the center of my undivided attention," he teased back.

"Yeah, it was nice," she agreed, but now she sounded sad.

"You can get used to that again, I'm not going anywhere. And speaking of, how about I make you some of my killer homemade soup, then you can take a hot shower and go to bed. I'll sleep in here on the couch."

"You're not staying here tonight." Her smile gone now, she frowned at him.

"There is no way in hell I'm leaving you alone after what you've just been through."

Like a switch had been flipped, she all but launched to her feet, her hands clenched in fists at her sides. "You didn't have any problem leaving me last time after I'd just been through hell," she screeched at him.

"I shouldn't have left you then, and I have no intention of making the same mistake twice."

Tears streamed down her cheeks, and she was vibrating with fury. "It's not up to you. Get out. And don't come back. We're not together anymore, Will, and I don't want you here."

"Too bad." It wasn't that he wanted to upset her further, or that he liked seeing her fall apart like this, but he had a feeling that this was exactly what she needed. She'd been burying these feelings for two long years, and she had to get it out so she could finally start healing.

"Too bad? *Too bad*?" Her voice was a high squeak that he could hardly understand now. "You don't get to say things like that to me. I needed you. I needed you to be there, to hold me, to tell me everything would be okay even if we both knew that it wasn't. But you weren't there. You left me. You left," she sobbed. "I hate you for leaving. I hate you for not being there for me. I hate you for being selfish. I hate you for doing what you wanted without giving any care to what I needed."

Will couldn't say that her words didn't hurt him because they did, mainly because they were true. He had left her, he had been selfish, he had prioritized what he needed over what she needed.

He hated himself for hurting her too.

"Let it out, baby," he urged.

"Don't baby me. Don't act like we're still together. We're not, Will, because you ruined what we had. You were never there, I know you loved your job and I never begrudged you that, but after all those years together you never wanted more, you never loved me the same way I loved you, your job always came first, I kept thinking that would change, but it never did. Just go, I can't deal with what happened last night and you. Things are over between us, you need to accept it."

Her body shook so badly that he thought she would collapse. He was seconds away from reaching out to her, but she dropped down onto the couch, curled in on herself, and sobbed her heart out.

He ached to take her in his arms, hold her, kiss away the pain he'd caused her, and yet he knew that she wouldn't welcome his touch. Did she really believe that he loved his job more than her? Looking back, he could see how she had come to that conclusion, but it crushed him. He'd failed her in even more ways than he had realized.

Eventually, Renee's sobs quietened, and she stopped trembling as her exhausted body gave out and she fell asleep. Now that she was out, he gave in to the need to touch her and squatted beside the couch, brushing her hair off her wet cheeks.

Not wanting her to wake with a crick in her neck or muscle cramps from sleeping curled up on the couch, Will very carefully gathered her into his arms. Carrying her upstairs to her bedroom, he pulled the covers back, then set her down. He pulled off her shoes but decided it was best to leave her clothes on, so he covered her with the blankets and tucked her in.

Then he stood and stared down at her. Tear tracks on her cheeks, red, puffy eyes, bandages on her head, and her neck where the rope had torn at her skin, to him she was still the most beautiful thing he had ever seen. Now that she had finally let go and stopped trying to keep her emotions under wraps, he prayed that she could find a way to forgive him.

They were balancing right on the edge.

If things fell the wrong way, when she woke in the morning she would tell him to get out of her life, that he had hurt her too badly to ever repair the damage, and he would have no choice but to walk away.

If things fell the right way then when she woke in the morning, the cobwebs between them would have cleared away, and they could finally work on healing and fixing what his decision had broken.

Stooping, he touched a kiss to Renee's forehead. "Sleep well, Little Bird, I'll be here in the morning. I'll always be here for you, I won't ever make the mistake of leaving you again."

CHAPTER
Nine

August 7th
8:33 A.M.

The first thing Renee realized when she woke up was that she felt lighter.

Surprised to see sunlight streaming around the corner of the curtains, she leaned sideways to check the time and was startled when the display on her alarm clock said it was after eight-thirty in the morning. It had been around six-thirty when she'd gotten home last night, which meant she had been asleep for nearly fourteen hours.

She never slept that long, and she never slept this late, but her body had needed it.

Not just her body.

Her mind too.

Renee winced as she remembered what had happened when Will had brought her back to her mother's house. She thought she'd moved past the stage of being angry with him for leaving, but obviously she'd been wrong, she very clearly still had unresolved anger toward him. That unresolved anger had come bursting out of her last night. She just remembered snapping. It was like somehow the lid that she'd thought she had latched tight had come undone and everything she had fought so hard to keep under control was let loose.

Since the last thing she could recall was sobbing on the living room couch, feeling like her body would be ripped apart by pain and despair, she had to assume that he had carried her to bed once she finally passed out.

Stretching, she threw back the covers, may as well get up and face whatever today held. As nice as it would be to cower under the covers, hiding from the world, she couldn't hide from her mind and the memories of her attack that were stuck in there.

Not feeling like a shower yet, she stripped out of the clothes she'd slept in and threw on a pair of leggings and an oversized t-shirt, then headed down to the kitchen, needing something to eat to refuel enough to figure out what she would do next. While she'd wanted to prove to herself that she could come back here, cats or no cats, she wasn't sure that she could stay here alone until her mother came back. That left her with two options. Either she could take Maggie up on her offer and stay in town at the hotel, or she could head back home, she'd just have to take the cats with her wherever she went.

Neither option was particularly appealing.

If she stayed here, she had to be constantly on the lookout for Will so she could avoid having to interact with him. If she went back home, she had to face the grave mistake she had made in getting a violent killer off, leaving him free to roam the streets.

It wasn't until she was already down the stairs that she realized she wasn't alone.

Her heart jumped into her throat.

Adrenaline spiked.

She opened her mouth to scream.

And then she saw who it was.

"Will? What are you doing here?" she asked.

"Told you there was no way in hell I was leaving you alone, sweetheart." He was standing leaning against the kitchen counter, an easy smile on his face. He was wearing nothing but a pair of gray sweatpants, hung low on his hips, and her eyes couldn't help but rove over his cut body.

"You stayed here last night? On the couch?"

"I've slept in plenty worse places, believe me. You feeling better?"

"Yeah, I am." She smiled back at him. She hadn't expected to find him here, especially after what she'd said to him last night, but that he had stayed because he didn't want her to be alone touched her. Things had gotten so messed up between them, and Renee knew that she wasn't without blame. There were a lot of things that she could have done differently, but she'd been hurting too badly to see past that.

"What's going on in that pretty head of yours?" Will asked as he walked toward her. He moved behind her, his hands went to her shoulders, and he began to massage them, working out the kinks and tension she hadn't even realized were there until he touched her.

"Thinking about us," she answered truthfully.

"Yesterday, you said you didn't want there to be an us," he reminded her. His words were calm, and his hands continued to work on her tight muscles, there was no anger in his voice, but she knew that what she'd said had hurt him.

"I was hurt and angry and scared yesterday."

He froze for a millisecond. "Does that mean today you feel differently?"

She considered that question. It wasn't an easy one. Her heart would always belong to Will, and she believed him when he said that he loved her. The problem was that Will leaving her had brought to mind issues she hadn't even realized she'd had before then. In the decade they had been a couple, he had been away more than he'd been with her, and while at the time she had believed he was just invested in his job—a job where he saved people—but that he loved her just as much. Once he left the doubt had crept in. If he could leave her that easily when she was so vulnerable, had he really loved her at all? Had he spent more time away than with her because he didn't really want to be with her?

"What are you thinking, baby?" he asked, his lips touching a light kiss to her neck. "Sweetheart, did you really believe that I loved my job more than you?" From the tone of his voice if was clear the idea was abhorrent to him, tearing him apart from the inside out.

"Not at the time. When we were together I knew that you loved your job but that you loved me too. But after, when you left so easily, I doubted everything. You know what life was like for me as a kid with my parents, they were hot and cold, sometimes they wanted us so much they were vicious, and then they lost interest, and they didn't care about us at all. You were gone so much, and it was okay because I knew one day you'd come back and we'd have the family I wanted, but every time you came back you left again. I started to wonder if you loved me the same way I loved you."

"It wasn't easy, Little Bird, leaving you was never easy." The deep-seated pain in his voice told her that was true.

Now that she had started talking, examining the emotions and fears that she had hidden from for two long years, she couldn't seem to stop. "Even when you were home you kept things from me, I got that it was your job, but after you left that last time I wondered if maybe you were only pretending to love me, and really you had this whole other life somewhere else, a life that I wasn't a part of, and that was why you left."

"Renee, *you* are my life."

"I was, but then things changed. *I* changed. I felt dirty, disgusting because of what he did to me. I blamed myself for not being smarter, not fighting harder. It was easy to believe that you walked away because you didn't want to be around someone who was broken."

"You were never broken," he said fiercely. His hands left her shoulders to grip her biceps, and he swung her around to face him. "You fought, even in that hospital bed you were so strong, giving the cops that drawing of the tattoo. I was so proud of you, baby." He reached up and caught tears with his thumb that she hadn't even known were falling. "I hate that he made you feel dirty. You are the sweetest, kindest woman I know with the biggest heart who wants to see the good in everyone."

Taking her face between his hands he kissed her, and in that moment she knew.

She had two choices.

She could hold on to her anger and fear, lock the man she loved out of her life. Or she could accept his apology and acknowledge that he had made a mistake and be happy with him by her side.

"I don't want to let you go," she whispered against his lips. "After last night I feel like I finally let go of all the fear and anger I had toward you, and at that man, and at myself. I feel so much freer this morning, which made me realize that I'm lucky to be alive. Twice I could have been killed, but I wasn't, I'm alive, and I want to live. Without you in my life I'm not really alive. I know that we have issues we need to work out, things we need to talk through, and it will take time to rebuild trust and the foundation that we need if we're going to move forward, but I want to, Will. I want us to move forward, I want to find a way to get back what we lost. I love you, and if you'll have me, I want you to be mine again."

∼

9:02 A.M.

How long had he been waiting to hear that?

How many times had he dreamed of hearing Renee say those very words to him?

Will had been starting to doubt that it would ever happen. Renee had been hurt too deeply. The mistake he had made was too big, too much had happened, too much trauma, too much pain, there was no way they could rebuild trust and get back what they'd had.

But now Renee saying those very words to him.

She forgave him.

She wanted to find a way to move forward.

She wanted them to be together again.

Renee shifted uncomfortably, hurt and confusion in her face. "Uh, Will, can you say something please? You're scaring me."

"Scaring you?"

"Before you said that you wanted me back, but now when I say it's what I want too you just stand and stare at me. Did you change your mind? Is it because of last night? I'm sorry about the things I said to you …"

"Don't be sorry, Little Bird." His thumbs stroked her cheekbones, and he leaned forward and kissed her forehead. "I'm glad you finally let that out, it wasn't healthy for you to be holding all of that in, and I don't ever want you to hold your emotions in like that again, maybe if …"

"Maybe if I'd let that out two years ago then we would have stayed together," she finished what he'd been going to say.

"Maybe, but, Renee, you had just been through hell, been hurt in the worst possible way, and I hurt you further by not being there for you. What happened is on me, and it's something that I won't ever forgive myself for, but if you're willing to give me a second chance, then I will spend the rest of my life proving to you that I will never let you down again. I love you, Little Bird, and there is nothing I want more than to have you back."

Tears welled in her eyes, but she was beaming up at him so he knew that they were happy tears. "I love you too. I missed you so much, Will. Even when I was angry and hurt I missed you. When you're not there, I feel lost … alone … swirling in a storm with nothing to anchor me. I need you, and I'm sorry it took me so long to realize it."

"Part of that is my fault, I was gone so much, and even when I was home with you, you're right, I was always keeping secrets from you."

"I never resented you for not telling me about what you did when you were working."

"I know, but I shut you out to protect you from that life, and instead you felt that you were being shut out. Come here." Will took her hand and led her to the living room. Taking a seat on the couch, he tugged her down onto his lap. "What was the first thing you always did when I would come home?"

"Strip you naked and check for new marks that weren't there last time I'd seen you, then I'd kiss every one of them, and then we'd make out." She tilted her head up and touched her lips to his jaw, nibbling on him then touching her tongue to his skin.

"Renee," he groaned. "You keep that up, and I'm going to throw you down on the couch and ravage every inch of your body."

"Is there a problem with that?" she asked coyly.

"No, Little Bird." He laughed at her. "But first I want to share something with you. I want you to know that any distance you thought was between us wasn't for the reasons you thought. It wasn't because I didn't love you, it wasn't because I didn't plan to spend my life with you, it wasn't because I didn't want to marry you and have babies with you. Sweetheart, the reason I shut you out of certain parts of my life wasn't just because most of what I did was classified, it was because I didn't want it to taint you. I saw people, friends, men I loved like brothers, blown up in front of me, I heard their screams as they died or as they lay there injured and afraid. I killed people, more people than I like to think about. I had to do things that I can't forget."

"I'm sorry," Renee whispered, nuzzling his neck while her hands stroked his chest.

"You were my light in the dark. You were the reason I made sure that I did whatever was needed to come home. Remember the time I came home, and there were scars on the soles of my feet?"

"Yes," she replied in a small voice.

"My team and I were captured once, tortured while rescuing two American girls who had been abducted while doing aid work. Two of my men didn't survive. The only thing that kept me fighting when I thought I was going to die was you. Needing to get home to you, not being able to accept that when I said goodbye to you before I left, it would have been the last time I ever saw you. I refused to leave this earth until we had lived a long life together and we were both old and gray."

"I almost lost you," Renee whimpered, pressing closer.

And that time was just one of many that he had cheated death.

The trembling in Renee's body was exactly why he had closed off that part of himself and his life when they were together, he hadn't wanted to expose her to it. But in trying to protect her, he'd given her the idea that he wasn't fully committed to them, which couldn't have been further from the truth.

Tipping her face up, he touched kisses to her forehead, her cheeks, her lips, anywhere so long as his lips were on hers. "Baby, you are every-thing to me. The most precious thing I have, you're my heart, my soul, my life. These last two years without you have been hell, I wanted to come to you so many times, but I didn't want to cause you more pain. But now you're here in my arms, and you're willing to give us another shot, and all I want to do is be inside you, feel you, touch you. I don't think I can wait any longer to join our bodies together."

"I don't want you to," she said, her hands curled in his hair as she kissed him.

Celebrating their reunion wasn't going to be hot, quick sex on the couch. He was going to do this right, take his time, make love to her and make sure she knew once and for all that she was the number one in his life.

Without breaking the kiss, he scooped her into his arms and stood with her, carrying her upstairs to the bedroom where he laid her down on the bed, then took a moment to just drink in the sight of her. Swollen lips, chest heaving as her breathing was heavy with desire, eyes bright and shining with need, she was perfection, and she was his.

"Will," she urged, her body moving restlessly.

"Patience, Little Bird," he admonished with a grin. "I want to take my time."

"I don't." She huffed.

"Tough." He laughed.

Before she could utter another protest, he crushed his mouth to hers as his fingers lightly traced the sensitive skin on her stomach, inching slowly toward her breasts. He hadn't been joking when he said he intended to take his time, he had two long years to make up for and intended to make sure she came several times.

Renee sucked in a breath when his hands finally touched her breasts, and when he began to tease her nipples she moaned into his mouth. Just touching Renee was enough to have him almost coming. Shoving his own needs down, he focused on Renee, she needed this, deserved this, and he wanted this to be something she would never forget.

"Lift your hips, baby," he murmured as he trailed a line of kisses along her shoulder. She did as he asked and he shoved her leggings and panties down her legs as the trail of kisses moved down her chest, pausing to minister to each of her breasts, drawing moans and sighs out of Renee as he went.

He continued down her stomach, but when he gently nudged her legs apart and settled between them she froze, her body going tense, and immediately he stopped.

"Baby, you okay?"

"I am, it's just ..."

"You haven't since that night," he finished for her so she wouldn't have to say the words.

"I couldn't, I didn't want to, it had to be you but we weren't ... have you been with anyone since we broke up?" The vulnerability in her eyes and the apprehension in her voice almost made his eyes tear up.

"Baby, there has never been anyone but you. You're my one and only." They had been together since they were teenagers and he had never once lusted after another woman. "But if you don't want to do this yet that's okay, we can just lie here together, or we can go grab some breakfast, or do some gardening, or anything you want."

"You, Will," she said simply. "I want you."

~

9:23 A.M.

"Are you sure?" Will asked her.

In her heart she knew she had never been more certain of anything in her life. "I'm sure, I just needed to know if you'd been with other women since we broke up. I wouldn't have held it against you, I just needed to know."

"It's only ever going to be you, sweetheart." He pressed a kiss to her bare stomach, and then one impossibly light one to her center where she was crying out for him, but he didn't give her enough to let her come, just kissed her once before turning his head and touching his lips to her thigh. Will kissed his way down one leg to her ankle, then changed sides and kissed her other leg from ankle back up to her thigh. Then finally, *finally*, his mouth was touching her where she needed him.

Renee cried out as his tongue and teeth teased her, winding her tighter and tighter until she couldn't even imagine how she would handle unraveling when she finally exploded.

When he added his fingers, stroking deep, it took her exactly ten seconds before she was spiraling along wave after wave of pleasure. It seemed to go on and on forever, and by the time she finally floated back down to earth she was trembling, her muscles spent.

"I don't think I've ever seen you come that hard," Will said, voice smug, a satisfied smile on his face.

"It's been two years," she reminded him, rolling her eyes at her man. He could be the sweetest man in the world, but he was a SEAL, an undercover cop, an alpha at heart, and he was never so pleased with himself as when he had her weak and trembling in the bedroom, her mind and body sated by what he did to her.

"It has. Two *long* years," Will added. He moved up her body and asked, "Condoms?"

"I'm on the pill, and neither of us have been with anyone else since we broke up. I don't want anything between us, I want to feel every inch of you inside me." Renee reached for his face and pulled it up to meet hers. She wasn't scared of having sex again for the first time since she'd been raped, although she would have been with anyone but Will. She wanted his lips on hers, his hands touching her body. What that man had done to her was just the physical act of sexual intercourse on an unwilling participant. This was making love and her mind and body needed to remember that.

Will's mouth never left hers as he eased slowly into her body, giving her time to adjust to his size. Once their bodies were joined, it was like the final hurdle she needed to overcome, to finally start moving forward with her life, cleared and behind her, and let herself go completely into the moment.

Their hands explored each other's bodies, getting reacquainted, they moved with the perfect harmony of two people who had been together for a long time, and it wasn't long before she was hovering right on the precipice.

"You first, baby," Will said as he reached between them and touched her most sensitive spot, hurtling her over the edge until she was freefalling. He came a second after her and together they soared through the heights of ecstasy.

Will touched his forehead to hers, and she wrapped her arms around his neck as tears began to tumble down her cheeks, her emotions felt like they were on overload.

"Heads up, babe, no guy wants to see the woman he just had amazing sex with burst into tears, it's bad for their ego," Will teased as he pulled out of her and dragged her into his arms.

Renee swatted at him. "Hey, buster, you didn't do that alone, I think we both made that amazing."

"Can't argue with that, beautiful." He positioned her so she was lying on her side with his arms around her and her head on his chest, his hand stroked her hair, the movement soothing. "Why the tears, Little Bird?"

"I just feel overwhelmed."

He stiffened beneath her. "You regretting what we just did?"

Renee lifted a hand and rested it on his stomach, her fingers tracing circles. "No, of course not. Not at all. I love what we just did. It's just that in the last twenty-four hours I've gone from thinking I would die, to letting go of emotions that I've been ignoring for years, to getting you back. It's just a lot to take in, but I'm happy. I don't think I've ever been happier than I am in this moment, lying here in your arms."

Will kissed her forehead. "Holding you like this is a dream come true. I've missed you so much."

"I've missed you too. Even when I was hurt and angry I missed you." A sense of nervous anticipation filled her stomach. As happy as she was and as much as she wanted to rebuild her relationship with Will, there were so many unknowns. She didn't live in River's End anymore, and did Will want to take things slowly or jump right back in to how things were between them before? Did she want to take things slowly or jump right into how things were between them before?

"I can hear you thinking. What's on your mind?"

"Just wondering what happens next. You know with us." Renee held her breath while she awaited Will's response. She didn't want to ruin this special moment, but her life had been thrown into turmoil too many times for her to be okay with not having a plan and knowing what was coming next.

"What do you want to happen next?"

"What do *you* want to happen next?" She threw the ball back into his court.

"How fast or slow we take things is up to you, sweetheart. You're the one who was hurt, and you're the one who nearly died." His hand moved to her neck where he gently brushed the bandages. "If you want we can date, keep things low-key, get to know each other again over the next two months while you're in town, and then reevaluate when it's time to go home. Or we can jump ahead, go back to the way things were before we broke up. You can move in with me, or I can stay here with you or split our time between the houses. I can look into transferring if you want to go back to your job after your vacation, or if you want to move here, then we can start looking for a new job for you."

The sensible thing would probably be to take things slowly.

They had been apart for two years, they'd both been through a lot in that time, and it was probably foolish to believe that they could just pick back up as though nothing had happened.

And yet she had lost two years with the man she loved, she didn't want to lose any more time.

"I want you," she said simply. "I don't think I can stay here in this house after what happened. And I don't think I want to go back to my job. Every time I walk in the door to our office all I'm going to think about is Josiah Holdsworthy, and I don't think I can do that. I want to be here because you're here, your job is here, and your family." Will had said that they could live together, which they had been doing before, but he still hadn't said anything about taking their relationship beyond just living together.

She wanted marriage and kids.

Did he?

Just like that her doubts were back.

"Our family," Will said.

"What?"

"When I ask you to be my wife they'll be *our* family."

Relief washed through her. Will *did* want the same things that she did.

"When I came back from that last undercover gig I had a ring, I was going to propose to you, tell you that I wasn't going to go undercover again, that I wanted to be there for you every day, go to sleep with you in my arms and wake up with you beside me. I've always loved you, Renee, and I will be proposing to you soon, and then we're going to live out our happily ever after. Now, unfortunately I have to get up and go to work. You should get dressed too, you're coming with me. You're not out of my sight for a second until we have this guy in custody."

With that, he kissed her and got up, leaving her staring after him. Will was going to propose to her, and she couldn't wait to find out how he would do it.

~

10:10 A.M.

"I can't come to the Sheriff's office with you every day," Renee said.

"We'll deal with each day as it comes," Will gave her a non-committal answer. If her coming to work with him each day and staying where she could be protected was what it took to keep her alive, he most certainly would insist that she come with him.

"That sounds like you've already made up your mind."

He shot her a grin as he parked the car outside the station but then sobered. "I need you safe, Renee, and I won't apologize for that."

"I wouldn't ask you to." She reached out and cupped his cheek in her hand. "But I don't want to live in fear again, I know what that's like, I lived like that for ten months and I don't want to do it again."

"I know, baby." Capturing her hand in his, he kissed the sensitive spot on the inside of her wrist, which made her shiver. "We'll find him, and until then I'll do whatever I have to to keep you safe."

Renee sighed, but then she offered up a smile. "At least this time I have you with me."

"Yeah, you do," he said, returning her smile with a sad one of his own. He wished that he had been there for her last time. Been there to soothe her fears, comfort her, reassure her, make her feel like she was safe when her world was spinning out of control. Wishing wasn't going to change the past, and at least he was here with her now, and he had a second chance to do things right this time. "I'm not going to leave you again, Little Bird. Ever."

"Good, because I won't let you." She leaned across the center console and planted her hands on his chest as she leaned in to kiss him.

This felt so good.

Not just kissing the woman he loved, but having her back in his life. This time he wasn't going to do anything to mess things up between them.

Reluctantly, he ended the kiss. The sooner they found the man who had tried to kill her, the sooner they could get to know each other again. And once they'd done that he intended to ask her to marry him. It bothered him that she hadn't been sure that he was as invested in their relationship as she was, and he wasn't going to make that mistake again.

"Come on, let's get inside. The quicker we figure out if Josiah is the man we're looking for and get him into custody, the sooner I can get you home and back into bed, we have a lot of time to make up for."

"Yes please," she said, her tongue darting out to lick her bottom lip.

"Renee," he groaned. "You do that, and I'm going to take you right here and now regardless of who might be walking past and see us."

Renee giggled. "Right about now I wouldn't even care if the whole town saw us."

"You're impossible," he said, forcing himself to undo his seatbelt and climb out of the car. "Wait there for me to come and get you."

Will didn't think it was likely that Josiah—or whoever the would-be killer was—would be watching the Sheriff's office and try to take her out. This guy seemed to like up close and personal games, a bullet to the head or heart didn't seem like something that would appeal to him.

Once he opened her door for her and helped her out of his truck, hand in hand they walked inside.

"Hi, Renee," Poppy said, jumping up from her chair behind the reception desk to rush over and give Renee a hug. "I'm so glad you're okay."

"Thanks," Renee said, and after a brief hesitation returned the other woman's hug.

"I've been overlooked I see," Will said, throwing in a dramatic sigh. "No hello for me today, Curly." He ruffled Poppy's curls. She was like a little sister to him and the rest of the guys, well, everyone except her boyfriend, Beau.

Poppy playfully punched him in the shoulder before standing on tiptoe to kiss his cheek. "Hello, Will," she said with exaggerated pleasantness. "Everyone is waiting for you. Renee, you need anything, coffee? Water? Something to eat?"

"I won't say no to a coffee," Renee answered.

"Lots of milk," Will added.

"Coming right up," Poppy told them.

Will led Renee through to the conference room. His brother Julian took one look at them holding hands and said, "You two are back together."

"We are," he said, trying not to grin too big because he knew his brother would kill for different circumstances that would give him a second chance with the woman he had loved and lost, and he didn't want to rub his happiness in Julian's face.

"Congratulations." Julian grinned, and he knew his brother meant it. "I'm happy for you two."

"Ditto." Fletcher was also smiling at them.

"At least something good came out of this," Abe added.

"Amen to that," he said as he pulled out a chair for Renee and then sat beside her. "So what do we have so far?" he asked, gesturing at the whiteboard, which was filled with scribbled notes.

"No forensics at either of the crime scenes," Beau told him.

"Disappointing but not surprising. He's obviously planned this out, I mean you don't just walk into someone's house and do what he did to Amika or Renee on the spur of the moment, leaving forensics behind would be too elementary for someone like him," Will said.

"We were also considering the possibility that Mary Pino was this guy's first kill here in town," Abe told him.

Will's eyes widened in surprise. He hadn't thought of that but now that he did it actually made sense. "Raphael admitted that he knocked Mary out and drugged and kidnapped the kids, but he was adamant he didn't kill his wife. And the way she was killed, it would have taken a lot of effort to get that setup, and I'm not sure that a drunken Raphael could have pulled it off."

"It doesn't sound like something he would do," Julian agreed. "I would have expected that if he wanted to kill Mary he would have shot her, stabbed her maybe, beaten her to death, or perhaps strangled her. Setting up the metal bar in the ceiling and leaving her to try to fight to stay alive seems too sophisticated for him. At the time we had no reason to believe that it could be anyone else, but now that someone did something similar to Amika and now Renee, I think we have to look closely at the idea that Mary is victim number one."

"So he goes after Mary to make a statement, we can assume he also told her he was here after a woman who had recently moved to town, but she died and couldn't tell anyone. He picks Amika next, and I'm sure he was happy that she survived and was able to tell us because he wants Renee—assuming she's the woman he's after—to know that he's here," Sydney said.

"I think he would have kept watch over Amika's house to see if she would make it out alive or not. Mary's house too, and probably Renee's. Do you remember seeing anything unusual when you got to her house yesterday morning?" Abe asked.

"No, but I wasn't paying attention. Renee told me the day before to stay away but I couldn't, and I was more worried about what kind of reception I would get when I got there and how I would convince her to hear me out." Renee reached over and took his hand, threading their fingers.

"Renee, why don't you tell us what you know about Josiah," Fletcher suggested. "I understand he raped and drowned several women."

She dragged in a breath, and from the way her hand tightened around his, Will knew she didn't like talking about this. "He didn't just drown them, he did something like what he did to me in the pool. He inserted a metal ring in his victim's bathtubs and then tied rope around the women's throats and tied it to the ring. He ran water in the bath, enough that they would have been able to hold their head out of the water but not indefinitely. He likes to watch people suffer." The fingers of her free hand strayed to the bandages around her damaged neck.

Grabbing her hand, he gently pulled it away and held onto it. "What did he say to you when you told him that you were going to make sure he went down for the crimes if he started killing again?" he asked her.

"He said he'd be watching me and that if he thought I was going to the cops I'd be sorry," she replied softly.

"If he saw you hanging out with Will and he figured out Will is a deputy sheriff then he could have thought that the two of you were conspiring to take him down," Beau suggested.

Was that true?

Was it his fault that Josiah had gone after Renee?

Guilt stabbed him sharp and hard.

"No," Renee leaned over and whispered in his ear. "Not your fault." Then she straightened and spoke to the room, "If this is Josiah, then he would have come after me sooner or later. He played me and used me to get him off, but when I told him that I would be watching him and would make sure he was caught and punished if he started killing again, that made me his adversary. He's rich enough that he won't ever have to work, he can go wherever he wants, do whatever he wants, and he won't stop. Killing me might buy him a little time, but sooner or later, he'll slip and get caught. And if he thinks that I told Will, then that makes him a target too. Have you had any luck in tracking him?"

"Not yet, but we will," Abe assured her.

"And until we do you're my shadow," he reminded Renee, putting his hands around her waist and lifting her over so she sat on his lap. "I won't lose you, I can't. I will protect you with my life."

To him, it was as simple as that.

If it came down to it, he would lay down his life if it meant keeping the woman he loved alive, but he prayed it didn't come to that. After everything they'd been through, they deserved to have their happy ending.

Hopefully, it wouldn't be stolen from them.

~

7:39 P.M.

Will froze as he walked into his cousin's office.

He and the others had spent the day interviewing neighbors of Mary, Amika, and Renee, to see if anyone could remember seeing someone hanging around. They'd had a few hits, people remembered a man sitting in a white van, but no one had remembered the license plate or had gotten a good enough look at him to give them a description. They had at least set up a meeting with Josiah Holdsworthy's family for tomorrow morning, hopefully they might know where he was hiding out or how they could find him.

Renee had been a great sport about staying here, even though she'd mostly been left alone with Poppy, and at least one of his colleagues at all times, while they went through scenarios and every piece of information they had. About an hour ago she'd disappeared into Abe's office for some peace and quiet, and she was now curled up on the couch fast asleep.

For a moment he just stood and stared at her. She looked so peaceful, so relaxed, the worry lines that he'd become used to seeing in her brow were smoothed, as were the tight lines around her mouth. Will hoped that once they had Josiah in custody, she'd be able to finally let go of everything that had been holding her back and move forward with a clean slate.

"She out?" Abe asked as he walked up behind him.

"Yeah, she's still tired from everything that happened the other night." Will knew it would take a few more good night's sleep and a few more days to chill out before she regained her strength.

"Don't mess things up with her this time," Abe warned. "You might not get another chance."

"I won't." He knew that he'd been beyond lucky to have this second chance with the woman he loved and there was no way he would ruin things. "I'm taking her to my place tonight, we'll be safer there because I have the alarm system, and besides I don't think Renee can relax at her mom's after nearly dying there."

"Call if you need anything," Abe said as he grabbed his laptop from the desk.

"I will. Say hi to Meadow from me and kiss my baby cousin."

Once Abe was gone, he walked quietly to the couch, not wanting to startle Renee awake. He crouched beside her and gently stroked her hair, letting his fingers linger on her soft skin. "Wake up, Little Bird," he said softly.

She stirred, lifting her head and blinking, looking sleepily up at him. "Hey," she smiled, "I don't remember falling asleep."

"You needed it," he reminded her. "Come on, let's get out of here. I have a surprise for you."

"A surprise?" she echoed, brightening and sitting up. Renee *loved* surprises. It was why most of the time he had never called to tell her when he was coming home from a mission or an assignment. He knew how much she loved it if he just turned up with flowers, or chocolates, or dinner reservations.

"Yeah, a surprise," he said, ruffling her hair affectionately. Taking her hand, he tugged her up and tucked her into his side as he led her outside. "You're staying at my place tonight," he announced, wanting to get that discussion out of the way first.

"Okay."

"Okay?" He'd been expecting an argument, it seemed he'd been wrong. "You don't mind?"

"I don't think I can go back to my mom's house again. I don't want to. I feel safe with you, and we have a lot to catch up on. I want to spend every second I can with you, so I guess I won't complain if you make me go to work with you again tomorrow, even if I only see you when you take a lunch break. So lets get the cats and go to your place."

As he drove, Will kept hold of one of Renee's hands, their fingers entwined, and just enjoyed being with her. Since they'd known each other practically their whole lives and been a couple since middle school, they were always comfortable together. Being with Renee felt like being home. In the dark, dangerous, and turbulent world in which he had spent most of his adult life, she was his safe place. While he'd been trained to always be aware of his surroundings and watch out for threats, he could relax, chill, let down his guard a little when he was with Renee. Living the last two years without her had been hell.

"Your house is adorable," Renee gushed when he turned into his driveway thirty minutes later. While he wouldn't call the house adorable, it was a quaint little white-washed cottage, three bedrooms, open plan living room, just enough yard that he could host cookouts in the summer and have all his family and friends come over.

"It's comfortable," he agreed. "Wait there till I come get you."

She rolled her eyes but stayed put until he walked to the back of the car to grab the cat carrier, then around to her door to open it for her. Because it had been so long since he'd had his woman back in his life and he had to be touching her at all times, he reached for her hand as they crossed the yard and walked up the porch steps.

Will knew the second that she'd seen her surprise because she froze and gasped, her hand tightening around his.

"Oh, Will." Her voice wobbled, and he was pretty sure that tears were only seconds away. Renee had never been much of a crier, but she'd had a rough couple of days—a rough couple of years—and now that she'd finally let her emotions out she couldn't seem to contain them.

Still clutching his hand, she turned in a slow circle, taking in the room. While he'd been at work today he'd called his cousin's fiancée Maggie and asked her to decorate the house for him. Christmas lights and tinsel decorated his living room even though it was only August. The table was set for two, with candles and crystal glasses.

"You were at work all day. How did you do this?" Renee turned to face him. The tears trickling slowly down her cheeks seemed incongruous with her smile, but he knew they were happy tears.

"I had a little help from a friend," he replied. Will set the cat carrier down and opened the door, letting the cats out to roam around his place. They meowed unhappily about their new living arrangements, but stalked off to investigate. Taking Renee's hand, he led her into the kitchen, and went to the fridge to pull out two bowls of spaghetti, and again Renee gasped.

"You remember that I like my spaghetti a day old."

"Unfortunately, this isn't quite a day old, but Maggie made it this morning when she decorated, and popped it in the fridge. And to drink we have sparkling apple cider."

"This is perfect," she said as she threw herself into his arms, kissing him fiercely. Wrapping her arms around his neck, she said, "This is our first date. You came over to my dad's house for dinner, I was fourteen and spaghetti was about all I knew how to cook. I wanted everything to be so special so I got out the fairy lights and tinsel. It was summer then too."

"This is kind of like another first date," Will said, keeping Renee held against his chest, her feet off the floor. "Only this time I'm not going to mess things up. This is our forever, Little Bird, and I thought it was only fitting that we start this part of our journey the same way we began the first part of our journey."

"Nothing could be more perfect." Renee kissed him again and lifted her legs to wrap around his waist.

Will groaned into her mouth. He hadn't been going to suggest sex tonight unless Renee had brought it up. Not because he didn't want to, so many nights since they'd broken up he'd dreamed about burying himself inside her, but tonight was supposed to be about reconnecting. This date fifteen years ago hadn't ended in sex, but it had been the night he realized that he loved her and she was his. He'd wanted tonight to remind her of that.

"You keep that up, babe, and dinner will have to wait," he said against her lips.

"Let it wait. I want you, Will, I *need* you," she pleaded.

That was all it took.

If his girl needed him then he would give her what she wanted. Carrying her through to his bedroom, he laid her down on the bed and couldn't help but think how perfect it was to have her back in his bed, this time he was going to keep her there.

"I don't think I can do gentle and sweet tonight, Renee," he warned.

"Good, I don't want you to. I want you to make love to me like I'm not a rape victim, like you're not trying to win me back, make love to me because I'm yours and you can't wait to have your way with me."

"You are mine, and after tonight you're never going to forget it."

CHAPTER
Ten

August 8th
3:42 A.M.

The house was quiet.

That kind of complete silence was synonymous with the middle of the night. Almost everyone—even the majority of the late-nighters—had crashed and gone to bed. It was too early for the early birds to be up yet, so it seemed as though the whole world was asleep.

This was the hour of killers.

Darkness reigned, people were at their most vulnerable in sleep, and it was free and easy pickings.

Just the way he liked things.

This was exciting, he liked the adrenalin rush of breaking into someone's home and setting up a fun game. While he called it a game he doubted that his victims thought of it the same way. To them it was a horrible, slow death, which as far as he was concerned only made it more fun.

He liked to watch. Since he picked victims who were low risk and were alone when he found them, he didn't have to worry about anyone stumbling upon him still in the house. It meant he was able to hang around for as long as he wanted. He didn't necessarily wait until they were dead, but he certainly stood back and watched for a while.

The first woman, the one on the farm with all the kids, he had stumbled upon by accident. He just happened to be out there, trying to find a quiet place to hide out while he was in River's End, and he'd seen the husband—or boyfriend or whatever—beat her and take a bunch of sleeping kids with him, and he'd thought why not take advantage of an opportunity that presented itself. He'd had fun watching the woman's arms shake as she struggled to hold her body weight up. She'd lost her grip a couple of times before managing to reclaim it and cling a little longer, fighting a losing battle but fighting it valiantly.

Did he feel remorse for the suffering he had inflicted on her and the others?

Not really.

He was here to make a point, and he would make that point no matter how many people he had to kill in the process. The second woman he'd set up hoping that she would be able to break through the plastic bag and get herself free so she could deliver his message. After all, what was the point of trying to make a point if the object of your plan was unaware of it?

Well, Renee Miller had certainly got the message.

After the second woman, he hadn't been able to hold off any longer before making a play to kill her. He'd thought he had. How had the woman managed to keep herself afloat for hours like that, especially with a head injury?

It was irritating.

She should be dead, but since she wasn't, he would take out a few other people so he didn't lose his temper—or at least not let it control him—before he circled around and made another attempt on her.

If Renee Miller thought that she was leaving him behind by leaving town, she was in for a rude awakening.

There was no way he was letting her go.

They had unfinished business.

The woman had messed with his life, and he intended to pay her back with interest—no one messed with him. No one. And certainly not some stuck-up woman who thought she was better than she was. The woman was hot, he'd give her that. Her long dark hair and big dark eyes contrasted with her pale skin and made her have the whole Snow White thing going on. Her breasts were small but round and perky, and she had a sweet little behind. He almost regretted that he hadn't taken her while she was unconscious at her house the other day. If he got another opportunity he would take it.

Right now though, he had to focus on why he was here.

The first thing he'd done when he'd broken in here was to sneak into the bedroom and sedate the man sleeping alone in the bed. After going with a spur of the moment decision with his first victim, he'd been more careful with the second one, making sure that he followed her first to confirm that she lived alone. He'd picked her at random, just like he had picked this man at random. They'd met his only qualification which was their living situation.

After sedating the man, he'd gotten to work setting up his game. While he had hoped that woman number two—he didn't know her name nor was he interested in learning it—would survive, he didn't wish for the same outcome this time.

This game was similar to what he'd done with Renee, but this one would be inside, in the bathroom. Giving the room a last look over, when he was satisfied that everything was as it should be he headed for the bedroom. The man was still out, but according to the dosage he'd given him, he should be waking up soon. While his victim was a big man, he was bigger and stronger and easily able to hoist him up over his shoulders and carry him to the bathroom.

He had fitted metal cuffs to the bottom of the bathtub to keep his victim where he wanted him. Dumping the man in the tub, he shoved him to the side so he could fix the cuffs around his ankles. Then he lifted the man up, balancing him against his shoulder so he could affix a rope to his neck. He looped the rope around the rail that the shower curtain hung off and pulled on it until he had the man standing upright.

Now all he had to do was wait for the man to wake up.

Thankfully it wasn't long, patience was not his strong suit.

"Wakey, wakey," he called out.

The man groaned and then began to move about in an uncoordinated fashion. "What ...? Where ...?"

Not in the mood for twenty questions, he didn't bother answering them, just strode over and ordered, "Better stand up if you don't want to die."

"Who are you?" the man stammered as his wide eyes frantically surveyed the room, fearfully taking in the rope around his neck and the duct tape on his hands.

"You're cuffed to the bath, you're not getting out, I'm going to turn on the tap and let the floor flood with water, then I'm going to give you a hairdryer to hold. It will be plugged into the wall. You drop it, you go to heaven. Or hell," he added with a wink.

The man just stared at him.

He wasn't saying that again, so he simply turned the bath on and then the taps in the sink, and water immediately began to flow. It would take a while for the room to fill up, so he had to wait to give him the hairdryer,

A ten-pound dumbbell was taped to each hand along with a small plank of wood—both of which he'd put on the man when he'd knocked him out earlier—would make it hard for the man to keep enough pressure on the planks of wood the hairdryer rested on to keep it from falling. Even with the motivation of knowing that if he dropped the dryer into the water he would be electrocuted, the man wouldn't be able to hold on forever, sooner or later his muscles would reach the end of their rope and give out, and the hairdryer would fall.

Questions flew out of the man's mouth, the usual ones, why was he doing this, who was he, then came the begging and pleading and bargaining, followed by the insistence that he wouldn't get away with it.

He ignored it all, watching the steady stream of water that was slowly flooding the room. The sink was already overflowing, and in another ten minutes or so the bath would also be overflowing. Crossing the room, he plugged in the hairdryer then placed it on the piece of wood.

"Good luck." He grinned as he headed out of the bathroom.

The man would soon be dead, and when his body was discovered,

Renee Miller would know that her time was coming. He would punish her for what she had done, he would make sure that she suffered an excruciatingly slow and terrifying death. She would die knowing that she had brought it upon herself, she would beg for mercy, but he wouldn't show her any, she would scream and cry, and each tear she shed and each scream ripped from her throat would be a balm to his soul.

Revenge would be sweet.

~

9:07 A.M.

"Don't leave Julian's side for any reason," Will said into his phone.

"I know, Will, I'm not an idiot," Renee replied, but she sounded more amused than annoyed.

"Good because so far we don't know what this guy will do next. He's in town because of you, he followed you here. It's unlikely that he's just going to walk away and accept that you didn't die." He hated that he was leaving Renee behind today, but he and Fletcher were going to speak with Josiah Holdsworthy's family, and she couldn't be there for that. It wasn't that he didn't trust his brother with Renee's life, it was just that no one was as invested in keeping her safe as he was because no one loved her like he did.

"I don't want him to come after me again, I'll stick to Julian like glue."

"Well, you don't have to stick that close," he grumbled, not liking the idea of Renee plastered all over his brother even though he knew that wasn't what she'd meant.

That made Renee laugh. "Relax, Julian is practically just as much my brother as he is yours. Be safe today."

"You too. See you tonight. Dinner with my family is at eight, but I should be back before then, probably by seven so I can shower and change."

"Okay, I miss you already," she said softly.

"Back at ya, babe, but it's only for a few hours and then I'm all yours again."

"Not really, I have to share you with your family," she grumbled.

"Only for a few hours and then I'm going to take you home to bed and make out with you all night long," he teased.

Fletcher cleared his throat before he could say more and he frowned at his friend like it was his fault that he couldn't tell Renee in detail every single thing he was going to do to her.

"I gotta go, honey, I'll call you when we're leaving."

"Love you."

"Love you more, Little Bird." When he hung up and set his phone down on the dash, he turned to Fletcher. "You know one day you're going to be in love and I can only hope that I'm there to ruin hot phone sex for you."

Fletcher grumbled, muttering something under his breath, and Will had to wonder whether maybe he was thinking about a specific woman, but instead Fletcher said, "Something is bothering me about this case."

Instantly all thoughts of phone sex fled his mind. "What?"

"Josiah Holdsworthy was arrested and charged with raping and murdering half a dozen women, right?"

"Right," he answered the rhetorical question, they'd spent all day yesterday discussing this case, he knew that Fletcher knew the crimes the man had committed.

"Mary Pino wasn't raped, neither was Amika Chin. Renee wasn't either."

His hands curled into fists so tight his knuckles hurt as the word rape was used in the same sentence as Renee. Will forced himself to relax. Fletcher was right, she hadn't been violated this time, and for that he was eternally grateful.

"The original murders he killed them all the same way in the bathtub, but this time he used a swimming pool, a plastic bag, and a metal bar and rope. That's a big change in MO."

"Maybe things changed after he was arrested. He realized how close he'd gotten to actually being convicted for the crimes and decided that he should start changing things up. Or this is different, this is about Renee, we know that's why he came to River's End, he followed her there. This is about punishing her for standing up to him and telling him that she would do whatever she could to make sure he was arrested and convicted if he killed anyone else."

"Family house is just up ahead," Fletcher said as they approached a large colonial in an upscale neighborhood. "Putting the victims in a position where they were able to hold off death for a while, long enough that they could have survived if they were found in time, is unique to both sets of murders."

"I think he's just trying to throw suspicion off himself. If he replicates the same scene at every murder then he's basically drawing the cops a roadmap of his crimes, but if he mixes things up, we might not connect them. If it wasn't for the attacks on Amika and then Renee we would never have even thought that Mary was killed by anyone other than Raphael."

Fletcher stopped the car at the gate, pressed an intercom button, and announced them. They were buzzed in and drove down the long drive to park outside the house. Before they could even get out of their car an older couple was standing in the open front door.

"Mr. and Mrs. Holdsworthy?" he asked as he walked toward them.

"Yes," the man answered for the couple.

"I'm Deputy Black, and this is Deputy Harris. We spoke on the phone yesterday."

"I remember." The older man nodded. Josiah Holdsworthy II was a tall man, close to seven feet and thin as a pole. He had a full head of silvery gray hair and piercing green eyes. He was dressed in a light gray suit, pale blue shirt, and dark blue tie. Despite his outwardly calm demeanor, Will could feel the tension rolling off the man, there was no doubt he knew what they were here to discuss.

"Come in," Joan Holdsworthy said, ushering them into the house. The woman was also tall, probably five-ten or eleven, but looked tiny next to her husband. She was wearing a pale pink pantsuit, and pearls around her neck and in her ears, blonde hair streaked with white pulled into a neat bun at the nape of her neck. She was less calm than her husband, her hands constantly moving, fiddling with her clothes, twisting together, and twirling her pearl necklace.

They were led into a formally furnished lounge room where the

Holdsworthys took a seat on a cream-colored couch, and he and Fletcher took the one opposite, a coffee table with a chessboard built into it sat in between them.

"Have you heard from your son recently?" Will asked.

"Josiah or David?" Mr. Holdsworthy asked although it was clear he already knew the answer.

"Your oldest," he replied.

"We haven't heard from Josiah since he called to tell us that he had been found not guilty and to ream us out for not showing up at the trial," Mr. Holdsworthy replied.

"Why didn't you show up to the trial?" Fletcher asked.

"Josiah thought it was because I was worried about how it would affect the business," Mr. Holdsworthy told them.

"Was it?" he asked.

"No," Mrs. Holdsworthy said in a soft voice. "Josiah has nothing to do with the business, David is taking over for his father."

She said it like that explained everything. From what he knew of the family from what Renee had told them, Josiah had always been the "bad" son, the one who didn't get good grades, who didn't take things seriously, who drank too much, had sex with random women he picked up in bars, who wouldn't go to college and wouldn't learn the family business. David on the other hand was the "good" son, the one who followed the rules and the family's plans for him.

"Did you think your son was guilty of the charges brought against him?" Will asked.

The couple exchanged a glance. "He was found not guilty," Mr. Holdsworthy replied.

"That's not what I asked."

"Why does it matter?" Mrs. Holdsworthy demanded, fire flaring in her brown eyes.

"Josiah admitted to his lawyer after the trial that he had done everything he was accused of. Double jeopardy means he can't be retried, but the lawyer said she would use her contacts to keep track of any similar crimes and would see to it he didn't get off that time. That same lawyer was recently attacked and nearly killed by a man who killed one other woman and attempted to kill a third. That surviving victim said in her statement that the man who tried to kill her said he had followed a woman to town and was there to teach her a lesson. We believe that the man is Josiah and we need to know if you've heard from him, or you know where he might be or have a way to contact him."

"He hates us, we basically never hear from him. He has his trust fund, and that means he doesn't need anything from us," Mrs. Holdsworthy explained, a sad glint in her eyes. "I can give you his phone number, well the one we have anyway, he doesn't always call from the same number the few times we do hear from him."

Neither one of Josiah's parents had seemed surprised that their son had claimed he had indeed committed the crimes he'd been found not guilty of. If they knew that Josiah was capable of rape and murder, why hadn't they spoken up during the trial? If they'd gone to Renee and told her whatever they knew about Josiah that made them suspect he was guilty, he knew she would never have bought the phony video footage, supposedly proving he was somewhere else at the time of some of the murders.

"What can you tell us about him?" Fletcher asked.

"As a small boy, he was such a funny little thing, always happy and giggling," Mrs. Holdsworthy said with a sad smile. "That changed when he was two, and there was an accident. The nanny was distracted with David, he was a colicky baby, and Josiah slipped in the bath, hit his head, by the time she found him he wasn't breathing. Obviously we were able to revive him, but after that he wasn't the same. It was like we got his body back but not his soul. He was cruel to his brother. None of the nannies we hired could handle him. He was interested only in himself and what he wanted. Alcohol, drugs, sex, by the time he hit his teens that was all he cared about. We heard him a few times, with a girl in his room. He was never gentle with them, he liked it rough and he liked when they fought, when they screamed.

As much as he wanted to know more about Josiah at the moment there was one pressing question he needed to know if they had an answer to. "Do you know where he might be hiding out or what he might do next?"

"Josiah's trust fund was enough that he'd never have to work a day in his life and he'll be living in the lap of luxury," Mr. Holdsworthy told them. "He could be anywhere. Once Josiah sets his mind to something he won't be distracted. If he's set his mind to getting to this lawyer then nothing is going to stop him."

Wrong.

Josiah wasn't going to get to Renee.

He would stop him.

No one was taking his woman away from him.

∾

7:40 P.M.

Renee pulled her hair up into a ponytail, it was hot, and she preferred not to have her long hair hanging down her back when it was warm, but then she let her hair fall down. With her hair up it made the bandages around her neck seem more obvious. It hadn't been a big deal when she'd been in the hospital or hanging out at the Sheriff's office, or even today when Julian had stayed with her at Will's house, but tonight she was going out to a family dinner with the entire Black family.

Since it was summer, there was no way she could get away with putting on a turtleneck, that would draw as much attention to her neck as the bandages did.

It was unavoidable.

Everyone would notice them, and everyone would be thinking about what had happened to her. Since the Blacks were a military family they likely wouldn't be too fazed by the injury, and they knew what had happened to cause it, but what would strangers think?

People would stare at it.

They'd wonder who had hurt her.

Even when the wound healed it would leave horrible thick red scars, and being on her neck they would be noticeable to everyone she came into contact with.

Picking at the tape holding the bandage in place, she unwound the white gauze from around her neck and studied the mark. It encircled her entire neck, was about two inches thick and dominated her slender neck. It looked like some sort of macabre necklace.

Every time she looked in the mirror she would see it. Be reminded of what it had felt like when she'd been trapped in the swimming pool, desperately trying to make her limbs move even though they felt like they weighed a hundred pounds each. The fear, the exhaustion, the resignation that finally came when she realized she was going to die, all of that she would be reliving each time she looked at herself.

Tears brimmed in her eyes as her fingers gently traced the angry red wounds, and it wasn't long before those tears leaked out, and she was weeping.

All of a sudden strong arms wrapped around her, turning her and pulling her against a strong chest. Will kept one arm banded around her while his other hand smoothed her hair as he murmured reassuringly in her ear. She couldn't catch the words he was saying, but it didn't matter, it was the sound of his voice and the security of his hold that penetrated and ultimately soothed her.

"I'm sorry," she said when her tears finally dried up.

"For what?"

"Crying all over you."

Taking her hands, he led her out of the ensuite and into his bedroom, he sat on the edge of the bed and pulled her down onto his lap. "Renee," he started, voice serious, "I don't ever want you to hold things in like you did before. Letting your feelings fester like that prevented you from being able to move forward. I wish I'd been there to make sure you were dealing with things, crying, screaming, getting angry, whatever you needed. I'm here now though, and I'm going to make sure that you're dealing with what happened the other night, so I want you to promise me that you will *always* tell me how you're feeling and what you need, don't hide it and don't hold it in."

She had always been the strong one in her family, the one both her parents and her siblings had gone to when they needed someone, but rarely did anyone return the favor. It was nice to have someone here to take care of her for a change. "I promise," she said as she rested her head on his sturdy shoulder, glad he was here to help her carry her baggage.

"Good. I love you, Little Bird." He pressed a kiss to her forehead.

"Love you too. Thanks for being here."

"Always. We're going to get through this, okay?"

Renee believed him.

For the first time since that man had grabbed her and slammed her into the wall, she actually believed that she would be okay.

"Come on, we have to be at my aunt and uncle's house in ten minutes." He tilted her face up and kissed her again, this time on the lips, and she immediately curled her hands around his neck and brought him closer.

She'd missed this so much.

Just making out with the man she loved, it was nice, and she hadn't realized just how much she'd missed it until she had Will back.

"Renee," he groaned against her lips. "We have to go, everyone is expecting us."

"Okay," she said on a sigh.

"I should have said no to dinner so I could keep you here all to myself." Will nuzzled her neck, drawing out a moan when his tongue darted out to wet that sensitive spot behind her ear and he followed it up by blowing a puff of air against the now damp skin. "Maybe I'll call and cancel."

"No," she said, trying to shake off the aroused haze threatening to engulf her. "We should go, I'd like to see your dad again, and your aunt and uncle, and I haven't seen Theo yet since I got back to town."

"Fine," he groaned, stealing one more kiss before his hands spanned her waist and he lifted her and set her on her feet.

"I'll just pop my hair up," she told him. She may as well get used to the attention her neck would bring with people she loved and trusted.

"I'll rebandage your neck."

Will followed her into the bathroom and waited while she braided her hair, twisted the bottom part into a bun, then wrapped a fresh bandage around her wound. Then she grabbed her purse, Will got the salads she'd prepared this afternoon, and they headed out to his truck.

His aunt and uncle lived about five minutes away, and by the time they were parking in the street out front of the house, it was exactly eight o'clock. Renee was excited to see Sean—Will and Julian's father—

and Patrick and Tatiana—Abe, Levi, and Theo's parents—again, it had been too long.

Her enthusiasm damped a little when Will took her hand and scanned the area as he hurried her to the front door. For a little while she'd forgotten that there was a killer who had followed her to River's End and already tried to end her life once.

The door was flung open just as they reached it and she was pulled into a hug by Will's aunt Tatiana.

"Renee, dear, it's been too long," the woman said as she hugged her fiercely, then kissed both her cheeks.

"I just couldn't come back here," she admitted. She'd always loved Tatiana Black, the woman was the epitome of the perfect mother, the kind of mother she'd always wished hers had been.

"I understand, dear." Tatiana smiled and tucked a lock of hair that had escaped the braid behind her ear. "Come on outside, everyone is out back."

Taking her hand, Tatiana led her through the house and out into the yard she had played in plenty of times as a child. Everyone was milling around, Abe and Meadow with their baby daughter, Levi and Sydney, Theo and Maggie, Poppy and Beau, Sean and Patrick, and Julian. Minus Meadow and Sydney, who hadn't been around when she had been with Will, these people had always felt like her family, sometimes more so than her biological one.

The guys were laughing and cooking on the grill, the women were oohing and aahing over the baby, and everyone seemed to be having such a great time.

"You can go hang out with the guys," she told Will who had left the salads in the kitchen and was standing behind her, his hand on the small of her back.

"You sure?"

"Of course. I'm going to go and say hi to your dad, and then I'm excited to get to know Meadow and Sydney better, and it'll be nice to catch up with Maggie and Poppy. And I cannot wait to cuddle that little baby."

"Maybe soon they'll be a new little baby Black around," he whispered in her ear.

"We can start working on that when we get home tonight," she whispered back.

His eyes grew wide. "Really?"

"Were you kidding about wanting a baby?"

"No, I couldn't think of anything that would make me happier than to hold someone in my arms who is half me and half you."

"Then yeah, really."

"I love you," he said as he dragged her into his arms and kissed her like they weren't in the backyard surrounded by his family.

When he finally released her, cheers sounded in the yard, and she looked over to see that everyone was looking at them and clapping.

"'Bout time you two finally got back together," Theo called out.

Her cheeks flamed in embarrassment, but she couldn't help but grin at all the happy faces smiling at them. Theo was right, it was time that she and Will got back together. Renee knew in her heart that before now she wouldn't have been ready, her feelings had still been too raw. Will had fought for them, showed her that he did love her, and while it might have taken her a little while to believe it now she knew that he regretted leaving her just as much as she regretted him leaving.

They were together, they were planning their lives, and the only thing that could come between them now was a killer who had her in his sights.

CHAPTER
Eleven

August 9th
10:14 A.M.

"He's been busy," Sydney said as she surveyed the scene before them.

"He no doubt knows that Renee didn't die in the pool the other night and now he wants to make sure she knows it's only a matter of time before he comes back for her," Will said, more determined than ever that Josiah Holdsworthy III would never get his filthy hands on Renee. Everything was going back to normal. No, better than normal, everything would be the way it always should have been. He and Renee were back together, he was going to propose soon, and the two of them would get married and have a family. Renee was his number one priority, and he wasn't going to let anyone or anything hurt her.

"So far he hasn't let up, he's killing almost every day, it's not likely to be long before he makes his move," Sydney said what he'd been thinking. "Maybe he thinks if he keeps us busy enough that we'll be too distracted, there are only six of us working in the Sheriff's office, he might think we won't be able to keep Renee protected then he can get her."

"That isn't going to happen," he said confidently. "Renee is staying with me at night, and one of us will be with her during the day. If he's waiting for us to get sloppy, or thinks we're just dumb country deputies, then he is sorely mistaken." Between himself, his brother, his cousin, and his friends they had around a quarter of a century worth of experience in the military, and a further quarter of a century worth of experience in law enforcement. Sydney was the least experienced of all of them, and even she had several years under her belt as a cop. They had faced militants in war-torn countries, they had killed people, they had performed high-risk rescues and extractions, they had faced murderers and rapists and gangs, they could take some rich kid who thought that his money made him immune to justice.

"We'll keep her safe." Sydney laid a hand on his arm and offered him an encouraging smile. Then once again her attention returned to the body before them. "Unfortunately, no one was able to keep her safe."

Bailey Martin was the fifth victim in River's End and the third to die. When they'd been driving back from the Holdsworthy house yesterday they'd gotten a call that Ted Delores had been found dead in his bathroom, electrocuted when a hairdryer that was plugged in had fallen into the flooded bathroom. The fact that the man was chained in the bath, had dumbbells duct-taped to his hands which were duct-taped to planks of wood made it clear that this was no suicide attempt or accident.

It was murder.

And given that the man had obviously been holding a third plank of wood with a hairdryer on it between his bound hands made it clear that the murderer was the same one who had gone after Mary Pino, Amika Chin, and Renee.

Then just hours later, he'd broken into Bailey Martin's house. The woman was seventy-nine, a frail old thing, confined to a wheelchair. She'd lost her husband almost two years ago, and although she had four children, ten grandchildren, and two great-grandchildren, they were busy with their lives, and while they made time for her she was often alone.

Bailey Martin had been Mrs. Martin to him and the other kids in River's End as she'd been the school nurse. She's been sweet and gentle with them, caring for them with cuddles and stories when they'd been sick and waiting for a parent to pick them up, and tending to their wounds when they'd fallen and hurt themselves.

Now she was dead.

The killer had balanced her wheelchair at the top of a flight of stairs, with the stair lift that helped her get access to both floors of her house down the bottom where it couldn't help her. He had tied it in place at an angle so that the only way the elderly woman could stay in it was to hold on. Eventually—and her thin arms probably couldn't have held on for long—when her grip failed she would fall out of the chair and down the stairs. A younger, stronger person could have survived the thirty step fall, but the old woman's body was frailer than most. From the looks of things, she had broken her neck in the fall and died instantly.

They'd search the house, and the crime scene unit would be here soon, but he knew they wouldn't find anything either, Josiah never left any forensics behind. He and Sydney would interview neighbors, see if anyone got a good look at anyone watching, or coming or going from the house, but he didn't hold out much hope anyone had seen anything particularly useful.

His phone rang and he pulled it out, half expecting to see Renee's name on the screen, but it was Maggie Wilson's name instead. "Hey, Mags, what's up?"

"One of my housekeepers just told me that there was blood in one of the rooms," she announced without preamble. "I checked to see who was checked into the room and it was a single guy in his late twenties going by the name Jo Worthy. I texted Abe and asked him to send me a picture of Josiah Holdsworthy, and I think it's him. He's not here, I checked the hotel, and he's not anywhere on the grounds, but he was here at some point."

"The man is a vicious rapist and killer, Maggie, and you went looking for him?" he demanded, harsher than he'd intended, but he couldn't believe the man had been under their noses all along.

"I went carefully looking for him," Maggie shot back. "I wasn't going to confront him if I found him."

"He could come back at any time, Sydney and I are on our way there now, if you see him don't approach him. If he says anything to you just be polite but make sure you don't go anywhere with him, stick to the common areas where you aren't alone. Seriously, Maggie, I've seen photos of Josiah's rape victims and you fit the profile."

"Don't tell Theo that, he'll freak," she said, her voice strained. She was right, his cousin would freak out when he discovered that a serial rapist and murderer was staying at his fiancée's hotel, especially given the fact that Maggie was pregnant.

"We're on our way," he said, gesturing to Sydney and heading out of the Martin house. "Text me if he shows up."

"Okay," she agreed before ending the call.

"What's up?" Sydney asked as they hurried out to her car.

"Maggie found blood in one of her hotel rooms and when she looked up who the room belonged to it was someone going by Jo Worthy. She asked Abe for a picture of Josiah, and she said she thinks it's him."

"Is he still there?" Sydney asked as she started driving.

"No. Maggie checked the hotel, he's not anywhere."

"Theo is going to freak."

That made him crack a smile. "Maggie said that."

River's End was a small town, and it didn't take long until they were pulling up outside Maggie's hotel. They both hurried inside where they met a harried-looking Maggie waiting for them in the lobby.

"I haven't seen any sign of him," she told them as they reached her side.

"Can we go up to the room?" he asked. "I texted Abe on the way here, and he's sending Julian as well. We need to get a sight on him the second he gets back here because there are a lot of people about and we don't know how he'll react when he realizes this is over." Will had a bad feeling that it wouldn't be good. Josiah had fixated on Renee, and when he realized that he wasn't going to get her there was a good chance that he would try to take out as many people as he could and go down in a blaze of glory.

"I'll meet you in the room when Julian arrives," Sydney said.

Will nodded at her then gestured for Maggie to lead him to Josiah's room. "Julian and Fletcher will stay here tonight in Jo's room if we don't already have him in custody, and Beau will stay down near the foyer, keeping watch so we know when he returns. We'll try to take him in here to minimize the chances of anyone else getting caught up in the middle of this."

"I can't believe he's been staying here," Maggie said. "When this gets out I hope it doesn't impact badly on the hotel, we only just reopened after the fire."

The whole town had pitched in to help get the Honeysuckle Hotel back up and running after it was nearly destroyed in a fire that almost claimed Maggie's life. "I don't think it will," he assured her. "We'll keep the hotel's name out of things if we can, and I think the press will be more interested in the fact that Josiah went after the lawyer who actually got him off on the charges." That wasn't good news for Renee, and he hoped that the stress of the press hounding her—as he was sure they would—wouldn't be more than she could deal with.

"It's this room," she said, pausing in front of a door on the second floor.

"Did you go inside earlier?"

"Briefly."

"What about the maid who found the blood, did she touch anything?"

"No, all my staff know not to touch anything that could be a potential crime scene. If they see blood and there's no one there who needs medical assistance, then the protocol is to leave the room, lock it, and tell me immediately so I can call the cops. Do you think the blood belongs to his next victim? Do you think it's someone else staying here?" Maggie's brown eyes were as wide as saucers.

"You should start going through your guest list and see if anyone is unaccounted for."

Maggie nodded and hurried off back downstairs while Will opened the door. He was pleased that no one had disturbed anything so he could get a feel for what had gone down in here. The blood had to be from the next victim, and he thought there was a good chance Maggie was right and it belonged to another hotel guest.

The first thing that hit him was the smell—old, stale, musty air. Like the room hadn't been used in days. He'd have to try to get Maggie to pin down the last time he'd been seen. The bed was made, the bathroom door open, the puddle of blood was on the floor halfway between the bed and the door to the bathroom. There were no signs of a struggle indicating that Josiah had caught his victim unaware. They had to figure out who the victim was and where Josiah had stashed the body. Since the room looked like no one had been in it in days, he had to assume that this victim had been dead for days.

How had Josiah gotten them out of here? It was summer and the hotel was full, that meant there were a lot of people here so it wouldn't have been easy.

So far Josiah seemed to always have luck on his side. He'd gotten off for crimes he'd committed, he'd managed to remain under the radar, all his kills had gone smoothly bar Amika and Renee's, but the thing with luck was it didn't last indefinitely.

He hoped.

Because if Josiah's luck held, then Renee would die.

∾

11:37 A.M.

She tapped her nails nervously on the desk in Abe's office as she waited for her boss to pick up the phone. This morning, sitting in the Sheriff's office, wondering how many more days she'd have to sit here being babysat, Renee had made a decision. She wasn't going to go back to her job.

She couldn't.

Every time she walked in the door she'd think of Josiah, the mistake she'd made believing him and the people who had died because of that mistake.

Doing that would slowly but surely kill her.

For the first time in two years, Renee truly felt alive. She had her life back on track, she had Will back, their relationship was moving in the direction she'd always wanted, he'd told her he was going to propose, and they'd even talked about the possibility of babies in their near future.

Now that she had everything she had ever wanted there was no way she would risk losing it by putting herself into a situation that would have a negative impact on her mental health.

"Hello?"

The voice in her ear drew her attention back to what she was doing. "Hi, Ken, it's Renee."

"Renee, how's your vacation going? Ready to come back already?" Her boss sounded enthusiastic, he hadn't wanted her to take two months off, but she'd had the vacation time saved up, and she'd wanted to take it despite him trying to convince her to stay or take a shorter break.

"Actually, I'm calling to give my resignation, I won't be coming back at the end of my time off," she admitted. It was hard to give the job up, besides the incident with Josiah, she'd loved helping people who had been falsely convicted and needed help proving it. It was her dream job, and not knowing what was coming next was scary, but she had Will, and she knew they would figure something out. For now, this was what was best for them as a couple.

"You're quitting?" he asked, a hint of panic in his tone.

"You know about what happened two years ago, and while I've been here I realized I hadn't really dealt with it. I need time to work on moving on," she explained.

"Then take some more time, come back when you're ready."

"I can't. I'm sorry. Will and I reconnected while I was here and his life is here, his family is here, and this is where I want to be."

"I understand," Ken said with a sigh. "I don't like it, but it sounds like your mind is already made up."

"It is. I'll be up one day soon to get my things."

"All right. We'll miss you, Renee. Take care."

"You too." When she ended the call she let out a breath of relief. It felt good to know she didn't have to go back there. She'd wanted to leave ever since that day when Josiah had told her she'd helped him get off for crimes he was actually guilty of.

Now she would call a real estate agent, get her apartment listed, then maybe one day she and Will could go up and pack up all her things and bring them back here.

That she would be living with Will was a given.

There was no way he would let her get her own place even after Josiah was caught, so when she sold her place she wouldn't be using the money to buy a new one. Maybe she could put it to a different use. She was currently jobless, and while she knew that Will would be happy to provide for both of them, she wanted to have a job, contribute. The money that she would get from selling her apartment could be used to start her own firm.

Excitement buzzed through her at the idea. It had been so long since she'd been excited about anything that the feeling felt foreign. Foreign but great. Surviving the aftermath of her assault had meant turning off her feelings, locking them away, focusing on feeling nothing because when you felt nothing, you didn't have to suffer all the overwhelming emotions of fear, disgust, pain, and humiliation.

"You look happy, what's up?" Abe asked as he strode into his office. He'd received a phone call about an hour ago and disappeared, she'd hoped it was good news, but she hadn't seen him again to ask.

"Just making some decisions about my future," she replied. She didn't want to tell him she'd just quit her job before she got a chance to tell Will, he should be first to know.

"I'm happy for you, Renee, really." He rested a hand on her shoulder and squeezed. "I have more news for you that should make you even happier."

"Yeah?" She brightened at the notion. If they had a lead on Josiah, then soon there would be nothing left standing between her and Will and their future. She knew that there was no way he would propose before Josiah was arrested. He was a protector at heart, which was part of the reason they'd broken up in the first place. Will's need to keep her safe had led him to need to find and punish the man who'd hurt her instead of being there to help her deal with the emotional fallout. This time she knew he wouldn't be leaving her side for anything, he'd protect her, and then once the threat was neutralized he'd propose.

"Josiah was staying at Maggie's hotel," Abe told her, dropping down into his chair on the other side of his desk.

She gasped.

He'd been so close.

Practically right under their noses all along.

Then she realized exactly what Abe had said. "Wait. *Was* staying at the hotel? He's gone?"

"One of the maids found blood in the room and told Maggie. Maggie called me and asked for a picture of the man when she realized the person renting the room was called Jo Worthy. She checked the whole place, but he wasn't there. Will, Sydney, and Julian are there now but so far no sign of him."

Her shoulders slumped. So Josiah had been here in town, but now he could be anywhere. To her, it seemed like they were no further ahead than they had been, although now she supposed they knew for sure that it was Josiah who had followed her here and wanted her dead.

"Hey, it's good news, okay?" Abe reached over, his large hand taking hers and squeezing comfortingly.

"It doesn't sound like it. He's still out there." It was hard to remain positive with a threat hanging over her head.

"But now we know more about him. We know the alias he's using, we know that he was in the hotel which means that people saw him, probably talked to him, we might be able to find out more about his movements while he was staying there. He used a credit card so we'll be able to track where he's been while he's been in town. We can use that to look for patterns, predict where he might go. Julian, Fletcher, and Beau will be staying at the hotel tonight, hopefully he'll be back there, and they'll be able to arrest him, but even if he doesn't return we're onto him now. We'll get him, Renee, that's a promise. You're family, and the Black family takes care of its own."

Abe's words reassured her a little. It sounded like he had a plan, and he and the others were all experienced, they knew what they were doing, she just had to trust them to do their job. "Okay. I know you guys have got this."

"Good." He smiled at her. "I know this is hard for you, having to hang out here all day and have one of us with you at all times, so even though you need to stay here I have a little surprise for you. Come on in," he called out.

The door opened and in came Meadow with baby Dawn in her arms, followed by Tatiana. "We brought lunch including some of Meadow's homemade cupcakes with cookie dough frosting," Tatiana announced as she held up a picnic basket.

This was exactly the distraction she needed right now. Time to get to know Meadow better and reconnect with Tatiana, who had been like a second mom to her. "Thanks for coming by."

"Of course." Tatiana waved off her gratitude. "I love Will and Julian just as much as I love my own, I practically raised them after their mother died, and I'm so happy to see you and Will back together and happy again. He hadn't been the same without you, dear."

Even though Tatiana wasn't her mother, or Will's, the woman had always been there for both of them, and she regretted not reaching out to her before now. Life after their mother's death had been rough for Will and Julian as their father struggled with undiagnosed PTSD. While Sean had since been diagnosed and was getting the help he needed she knew that there had been violence in the house when he'd been at his worst. But Tatiana had been there, looking after the boys, having them at her house more often than not, and Renee had been on the receiving end of that same help when her parents had been too preoccupied with themselves to care about their kids.

She hoped that one day she and Will would be able to give that same kind of open, loving, caring family to not just their own kids but any others in need. They were on the right track, and they had the wonderful example of Tatiana to guide them, and looking at the little baby in Meadow's arms, she hoped that sooner rather than later they would start working on creating that family.

∽

4:34 P.M.

"Abe just got a call from Olive Tiggle reporting a car that has been parked out the front of her farm for a week now without moving,"

Sydney announced as she walked back into the room where their desks along with Julian, Beau, and Fletcher's were set up.

"Your face says it's more than just an abandoned car," he noted. Sydney's golden brown eyes were glowing, and she had a big smile on her face. An abandoned car usually just meant that someone had had a little too much to drink and then forgotten to come back for the car. It was summer, the whole area was teeming with tourists, and it wasn't uncommon for that to happen.

"Car is a rental and it's registered to Jo Worthy," she said as her smile grew bigger.

That had him shooting to his feet. "Olive's farm borders Mary Pino's place. If he dumped the car out there, he probably hasn't been back to the hotel since he killed Mary. And if he hasn't been back there since, then the blood there probably belonged to the real first victim. He killed someone before Mary, someone we haven't found yet."

"Probably also means that he isn't going to go back to the hotel," Sydney added.

Will agreed, as much as he didn't want to. "Fletcher, Julian, and Beau will stay there just in case."

"Abe wants us to head over to the car, see if we can find anything there that might help us figure out what his next move was."

Grabbing his keys, he tossed them to Sydney then headed for the door. "I'll say goodbye to Renee and meet you in the car." Sydney had been hanging out in Abe's office most of the day, he knew his cousin had filled her in on the fact that Josiah had been staying at Maggie's hotel, and he knew she'd been upset to learn he had once again slipped through their fingers. He'd wanted to hang out with her during his lunch break, but she'd been with Meadow and Tatiana, and he wanted her to start connecting—or reconnecting—with people here since he hoped she would be moving here permanently in the very near future.

"Hey," Renee said, standing and hurrying over to wrap her arms around his neck and hug him. "You heading out?"

"We have something we need to look into, how about I spring you from here when I get back?"

"That would be awesome." She grinned.

"Not sure how long we'll be," he warned.

"As long as when you get back we can go home, spend some time together, I don't care." She kissed him again, and his body couldn't help but respond to having this sexy, sweet, strong woman in his arms, but he shoved aside those thoughts, now wasn't the time. He could have her tonight, and every night after this, she wasn't going anywhere.

So long as he found Josiah Holdsworthy III.

Renee deepened the kiss, pressing her body right up against his, and this time he had to pull his lips away, put his hands on her shoulders, and physically put some distance between them.

"Baby, you can't kiss me like that when I'm at work. Especially not when my cousin is watching."

"I didn't see a thing," Abe said, choking on a laugh.

"I'll be back soon, I promise, then I'm all yours for the night."

"I'll be waiting," she said with a grin and a wink.

By sheer force of will, he turned around and made his feet carry him out of the room, then outside and into the car where Sydney was waiting for him.

"Has Maggie found any of her guests who haven't checked out, but haven't been seen and aren't in their room?" Sydney asked as she started driving.

"Not yet, last I heard from her everyone is currently accounted for."

"Employees too?"

"Employees too," he acknowledged.

"I have a bad feeling, Will," Sydney announced when they were about halfway to where the abandoned car had been reported.

Reluctantly he had to admit that he did too. Something felt wrong, off somehow like they were missing something important."

"If he followed Renee here then he must know the two of you are together and that you're the one who saved her. You should be careful, he might try to go after you next," Sydney said.

"I can take care of myself," he said quickly. It wasn't himself he was worried about, it was Renee. Yeah she was tough, and she'd taken self-defense classes, she knew how to fire a gun, but she was small, easily overpowered, and Josiah wasn't just playing with his physical strength he was playing this mentally smart as well.

"You can take care of yourself, but your focus is Renee, and Josiah no doubt knows that, he'll use it to his advantage because he knows that if he can get you out of the way then he'll have an easier run at Renee. At least that's what he thinks, but we all have your back. I know I'm younger than you guys, and I wasn't in the military, but you're all my family now, and if someone messes with one of us they mess with all of us."

"Thanks, Syd." He smiled at her. When he first found out who Abe had hired as the new deputy he'd been surprised, not because Sydney was a woman but because she was young, didn't have a lot of experience, was a city girl, and not used to the way small towns worked, but having seen her in action, he knew his cousin had made the perfect choice. "That means a lot to me."

"Of course." She nodded briskly. "We're a team and a family, and one day we're actually going to be family since I'm with your cousin. There's no way that any one of us will let anything happen to Renee. I really like her, and I know I don't know all the history between you two, but I'm glad you're getting a second chance."

"Trust me when I say I don't deserve the second chance, but I'm going to do everything I can to prove to her that she can trust me and that I'm worthy of her love. Starting with finding the man tormenting her and getting him off the streets."

"That we are going to do. He's already slipped up by not cleaning up the room before he left and giving us a clue, and then leaving the car here for us to find. He's gotten too cocky, thinking that he has this all wrapped up, and that mistake is going to cost him his freedom."

Or his life, Will thought.

Josiah Holdsworthy III had hurt Renee, made her feel guilty for believing the fake evidence he'd given her and getting him off on the crimes. He'd made her feel afraid and left her in a situation that very easily could have—and *would* have if he hadn't found her in time—claimed her life, for that he deserved to die.

One wrong move, one *hint* of a wrong move, and Will wouldn't hesitate to put a bullet between his eyes. It wouldn't be the first time he'd rid the world of a vile parasite and it no doubt wouldn't be the last.

"There's the car," he said, pointing up ahead of them when he spotted it.

"He probably picked this road for a reason, it's quiet, doesn't get a lot of traffic, and if he'd had an inkling he might have to leave the car behind then he probably thought it wouldn't be discovered for a while. Which it wasn't."

Unfortunately, when they'd searched the Russo property after finding Mary's body and were looking for the missing children, they hadn't come this far. If they had, maybe they could have avoided the other murders and the attempts on Renee and Amika.

The what-if game was a dangerous one, one he'd had to learn when he joined the military never led to anything good. You went down that road, and you might never come back. You got stuck—trapped—in a quicksand of guilt and second-guessing that could drag you down and suffocate you if you let it.

Sydney parked the car behind the one Josiah had dumped out here, and they both got out and walked over to the other vehicle. "Let's pop the trunk," he said. If Josiah had attacked someone at the hotel and brought them with him, he expected to find blood in the trunk. Blood and hopefully a clue as to who the mystery victim was.

Thankfully the car was unlocked, and he popped the trunk and then crossed to check it out.

"Blood," Sydney said as soon as they looked inside.

"We'll match it to the samples from the hotel and hopefully sooner rather than later we'll get a hit in a database so we can ID the victim."

Will was just straightening, intending to survey the area to see if he could figure out what Josiah had done after getting out of the car when pain exploded in the left side of his head.

6:20 P.M.

Something felt wrong.

Her gut was all but screaming at her that something had happened.

It wasn't helping that Abe had received a phone call a little while back, stormed out of the room, and not come back.

Renee knew he was still here in the Sheriff's office because there was no way he would leave her alone when there was a serial killer after her, but whatever had happened he was trying to keep it from her.

That only ramped up her anxiety.

She had tried to be patient, sit here and wait for Abe to come and tell her what was going on—because she had no doubt that this was about her and Josiah—she had even tried pumping Poppy for answers, but her friend didn't have any to give. Her stomach was a pit of nauseous energy, and her whole body was tight, she needed answers and she needed them now.

Giving up on waiting, Renee got up and headed out of Abe's office. She would find him and make him tell her what was going on. She had no idea how she would do that, he was twice her size, and despite the fact that he'd mellowed since she'd last seen him, she knew he was strong and determined and would do only what he deemed best.

Deciding pleading—begging really which she wasn't above at this point—was her best option, she had just thrown the door open and was heading out to find where Abe had hidden himself away when the door to the building opened, drawing her attention.

She expected to see Abe, having snuck outside to make his phone calls without her overhearing, but instead it was Will striding through the door.

Relief swamped her.

He was okay.

She'd been worrying for nothing.

Worst-case scenarios had been running through her head, each worse than the last. As someone who had been the partner of a military man and an undercover cop, she wasn't new to worrying about the safety of her loved one. But Will's job was safer now, he was a deputy in a small town, she'd thought her worrying days were mostly behind her.

Without thinking about it, her feet started toward him, but then she froze.

He *wasn't* okay.

There was blood on his short-sleeved gray shirt.

A bandage on his head.

"It's not as bad as it looks," he said, walking toward her.

She backed up.

Will was hurt.

He'd been hurt working this case.

He'd been hurt because of her.

Josiah was only in town because he'd followed her here. If she had stayed at home, Josiah would never have even known about River's End, and Will wouldn't be hurt.

"Renee, listen to me," he said, advancing on her even though she was shaking her head, holding out her hand, and continuing to back up. "I'm fine."

Was he crazy?

Of course he wasn't fine.

She wasn't blind, she could see the bandage and the blood.

He was hurt.

"You're not listening," he said as he closed the distance between them and wrapped his hands around her shoulders, giving her a small shake. "I'm okay. Here, see?" He took one of her hands and pressed it to his chest above his heart. "Feel my heart beating? Feel my chest rising and falling with each breath I take? I'm really okay."

He was alive, whether or not he was okay was yet to be seen.

"Wh-what happened?" she asked, entwining her fingers with Will's and lifting her other hand to feather her fingertips across the crisp white bandage taped to his left temple.

"Sydney and I were out by the Tiggle farm because there was a report of an abandoned car that turned out to be a rental that Josiah was using. When we got there someone took a shot at us."

Renee could feel the color draining from her face, and her knees went weak. If Will hadn't snapped an arm around her waist and dragged her up against him, she probably would have hit the floor. "You were shot?" she squeaked.

"Shot is a bad word, a bullet skimmed my head, I'm fine, didn't even need stitches."

"You're really okay?" Renee searched his eyes, looking for any signs that he was lying to her. He looked okay, and he was holding her tightly. His hands weren't shaking, and he wasn't wobbling like he was woozy.

"Perfectly fine. You ready to get out of here?"

"Yes." She shoved out a breath, forcing her wildly beating heart to calm down. "We should get you home and into bed."

"Honey, if I'm going to bed I'm not going to be sleeping," he whispered in her ear then kissed the side of her neck right above the bandages.

"You're incorrigible," she rebuked, but heat pooled in her stomach.

"Only with you." He winked, then began to pull her toward the door. He all but shoved her into the car, then flew around it and dived into the driver's seat, and she couldn't help but laugh. "Something funny, babe?"

"Look at you, running around like a caveman dragging me off to your cave for hot sex." She giggled.

"Dragging you off, huh? You don't want to be dragged off for hot sex?" He reached over and took one of her breasts in his hands, rolling her nipple between his fingers. She moaned, her head falling back as she thrust her chest forward without even thinking about it. "Kinda seems like you want to be dragged back to my cave for hot sex," Will said smugly, withdrawing his hand.

"Quit teasing me," she groaned, trying to grab his hand and bring it back so he could continue to minister to her breasts, but he wouldn't budge.

"Oh, I'm going to tease you. I'm going to tease you until you're begging me to let you come, and then I'm going to do it again and again until you can't think."

She didn't even know what to say to that, but her body responded instantly. She was tingling, restless, squirming in her seat, desperate for his hands to be on her body. Renee wasn't used to being this needy sexually. She'd been used to living with a man who was away for long stretches of time, and ever since she'd been assaulted sex had been the furthest thing from her mind.

But now she was counting the seconds until they got to Will's house.

All thoughts of the discussion she'd wanted to have on their future and her quitting her job flew from her mind, she was consumed with the need to make love to Will.

When he parked the car in his driveway, she waited impatiently for him to come around and get her. Will opened the door and picked her up, Renee wrapped her legs around his waist and immediately crushed her mouth to his, kissing him greedily as she pressed her center against his hard length.

Somehow he got them inside, and the alarm system armed without dropping her or breaking the kiss and carried her into the living room. He sat and put her on his lap, her legs straddling his, and she felt a sense of loss without him pressed up against her.

Before she could protest, beg him to put her out of her misery and give her what she knew they both needed, his hand was shoving her ankle-length white skirt up and slipping his hands inside her panties.

She moaned in delight as his fingers touched the part of her that was aching for attention, and then nearly lost her mind when he slid a finger inside her. His expert ministrations had her quickly heading toward the peak, but she held back. This was about both of them, and she wanted them to come together.

Somehow managing to form a coherent thought, she moved one hand from Will's shoulders and fumbled to get his jeans undone so her hand could get inside. She could tell from the way he stiffened he was going to tell her to stop, but she drowned out any protests he could have made by deepening the kiss.

When her fingers touched him, she nearly came then and there. He was so big, so hard, so hot, and she couldn't wait to have him inside her.

Will added another finger inside her, stretching her, stroking her deep, while his thumb kept up a steady pace on her little bundle of nerves. Her hand gripped him tightly, moving up and down his hard length. The closer she got to coming the faster her hand moved, and she could tell by the way Will was trembling that he was close to coming, but holding off because he wanted her to come first.

He pressed harder with his thumb, and she came apart. Her whole body shaking, Will's name ripped from her lips, as she came harder than she ever had in her life.

By the time she was cognizant again she was slumped against Will's chest, completely spent, her entire body feeling like jelly.

"That was out of this world," Will said.

"Yeah." She sighed contently, nuzzling her face against his neck.

"You ready to go again?"

"After that, I'm not sure I can."

"Honey, we have the whole night, you're going to come so many times you'll lose count." Scooping her up into his arms, he carried her toward the bedroom, and as much as she'd thought she couldn't come again so soon after that amazing orgasm Will had just given her, already her body was stirring at the thought of Will's mouth on her, and him inside her.

For a long time, she had wondered if she would ever be able to have sex again without flashing back to her assault. When she and Will had first come together a couple of days ago she'd been afraid that she would freak out. But the past didn't seem to matter when she was with Will. All that existed was the two of them, no past, no future, just the present, just the two of them in each other's arms, passion and love igniting between them.

Will represented both the best and worst of her life, her highest highs and lowest lows, but there was more good than bad, so much more, enough to wash away all the bad and clean the slate so they could have the most amazing future.

CHAPTER
Twelve

August 10th
1:39 A.M.

Something roused him from sleep.

Will focused, immediately trying to pinpoint exactly what had woken him. Years as a SEAL and years undercover had honed his ability to be aware of his surroundings even in sleep, and it usually took only the slightest sound or movement to snap him awake.

Now, he scanned the room, searching for whatever his instincts had sensed.

Nothing appeared to be out of the ordinary, they'd left the curtains open when they finally tumbled into bed for sleep and not sex, so there was enough moonlight for him to scan the room and everything looked as it should. Keeping his body relaxed and his breathing even—just in case someone *was* hiding in the shadows—he counted to one hundred, giving any intruder a chance to get complacent and move.

When nothing did move, he finally sat up, reaching for the gun he kept in the drawer of the nightstand, and was about to swing his legs over the side of the bed when he heard a moan behind him.

Renee.

It wasn't an intruder who had woken him, it was Renee having nightmares.

He turned, and the look on her face shot him straight in the gut. Her brow was furrowed, her mouth hanging open, fear etched into every single one of her features. She moaned again and began to thrash like she was fighting off an attack, and he didn't have to guess what she was dreaming about.

Another moan tore from her lips, and the abject terror in that one sound was enough to make his guilt soar. He should have been there that night to protect her, not away on a job that he knew Renee would have preferred he leave for something that would give them more time together. He'd been selfish, and Renee had paid the price.

Well, he was here now, and he would protect her from the nightmares as best as he could.

Leaning over her, he gripped her shoulders and gave her a firm shake. "Renee, wake up, baby."

She whimpered and fought his hold on her.

"Renee," he said more firmly. "You're dreaming, wake up now."

Tears leaked from the corners of her scrunched-up eyes and she cried out.

"Wake up, sweetheart, please," he begged, giving her another shake.

Her eyes snapped open, and she began to struggle against his hold like her life depended on it.

"It's okay, Little Bird." He pulled her squirming form against his chest, cradling her head with his palm and rocking her gently from side to side. "It's just me. Will. You were dreaming, honey, but you're safe, you're here in my house, in my bed. I got you."

"Will?" she said, voice shaky, and she was trembling violently in his arms.

"Yeah, honey, it's me. You're safe, okay? I got you, and I'm not letting you go."

She gave a sob and burrowed into him. Her skin was cold and

clammy, and she was still shaking, so he pulled the blanket free, wrapped it around her, and repositioned himself so he was resting against the headboard with her cradled on his lap. He gave her time to get it out, cry, believe that it had been nothing more than a dream and that she was safe now.

"You're safe with me, baby. Always, okay?" Will knew that she was only just learning to trust him again, and since he had failed her in the past he worried that she doubted his ability to protect her. Protection was in his blood, he came from a military family, his father, his grandfather, his uncle, his brother, his cousins, even his mother had been briefly in the military before she had him and Julian. Protecting people was what he did, and that he hadn't protected the one person who meant the most to him had eaten away at him for two years. It was why he'd gone undercover to find the man who'd hurt her to begin with. It was his way of atoning for his failings, but in the end, all it had achieved was failing her further.

"I know," she said, but her tears that wet his bare chest said otherwise.

"I swear to you, Renee, I won't ever let anyone lay a hand on you ever again."

"I never blamed you for what happened," she said, finally lifting her head to look at him. "Is that why you left? Why you went undercover to find him? Because you blamed yourself?"

"Yeah, baby." He touched his lips to her forehead. He didn't deserve this woman, and the urge to tell her that and send her away was strong.

But he couldn't do that.

It would be like cutting off a piece of his body and throwing it away.

That was how deeply she was ingrained in him.

She was a part of him, and selfish or not, he couldn't let her go.

"Will, if I ask you something, will you give me an honest answer?"

"Yes," he said without thinking, in this moment he would give her or tell her anything she asked for.

"The man who raped me, did you really just arrest him or did you kill him?" She looked up at him with big, trusting eyes and he couldn't help but tell her the truth.

"He's dead."

"You killed him?"

"Yes."

She hesitated, lifting a hand to wipe at her wet cheeks. "Painfully?"

"Yeah, babe, painfully. He paid for what he did to you." He wasn't going to give her details because she didn't need to know that he had beaten the man to a bloody pulp, then cut off his penis before putting a bullet through his forehead.

Renee rested back against him. She'd stopped shaking and thankfully her tears had stopped. They sat like that for a long time, not speaking, just sitting together, slowly healing from the trauma of Renee's assault by being together, drawing strength for one another.

"Thank you," Renee finally whispered. "I was angry with you for a long time, so hurt by you leaving. I won't deny that I needed you with me, but maybe I needed him dead too."

Her words eased the vice-like grip of guilt just a tiny bit. "You know I'd do anything for you, Little Bird. I wish I had been there with you though. Did you have nightmares a lot after it happened?"

"Some," she replied, the hand resting on his chest began to trace circles. "I know you called my family before you left and they came right away. My mom stayed with me those first few months, and I know she's flighty and self-centered, but she was actually really great."

"I'm glad you weren't alone."

"Me too. I wish you had been there, but everything worked out in the end. We're together again, and this time nothing is going to tear us apart." Her fingertips trailed higher until they brushed lightly across his lips.

"Nothing could make me leave you again," he said, his tongue darting out to capture her finger, drawing it into his mouth and sucking on it. "I love you so much that it hurts we lost two years together."

"I know. But it's time to look forward not backward. Now there's nothing standing in our way. Make love to me, Will."

He lifted her and laid her down beneath him. He was the luckiest man in the world to have earned her forgiveness, and he knew that in time he would earn her trust, once he did he would ask her to marry him.

Will was leaning down to kiss her when he heard a whizzing sound and then felt a sharp sting in his back. "What the ...?" he said, turning in the direction the sound had come from.

"Ouch," Renee squealed.

He looked down at her, and his heart practically stopped beating when he saw a small dart sticking out of her arm.

Someone had drugged them.

Will tried to move, get to his weapon, but his body refused to comply with his commands. His arms began to wobble, and he tried to roll sideways so his body didn't crush Renee's when he passed out.

The sound of the window opening caught his attention, and he turned to see Josiah climbing through his bedroom window. Then his eyes grew wide as a second man climbed through the window behind him.

"You," he said on a faint exhale.

"I think you were expecting him, but not me." The second man grinned.

This couldn't be happening.

They'd been wrong all along.

"He's served his purpose." The man grinned, then fired the gun he had pointed at Josiah Holdsworthy III.

The body fell to the carpet, sightless eyes staring straight at the bed in a sort of wordless sign that their bodies would be the next to fall.

His trembling arms gave out, and he slumped down onto the bed.

Beneath him, Renee's eyes fluttered closed, and his last thought before he joined her in unconsciousness was that he had failed.

He hadn't kept her safe as he had promised.

Instead, he had gotten them both killed.

He fought it, but oblivion claimed him anyway.

∽

2:43 A.M.

Hunter Ford tapped his foot impatiently.

To be honest, he hadn't expected things to go quite this easily. Will Black was a cop, and as such he'd assumed that the man would have at least a reasonable quality home security system. He hadn't known how he would gain access to the house. Hunter wasn't a smart guy, he wasn't a computer whiz who could figure out a way around the alarm system, and he wasn't much at acting, no way he could talk his way inside—especially not with a hostage. His talents were more a lack of conscience and an aptitude for killing with a knife.

Not something he had done a lot of these last several days.

For the sake of getting what he wanted, he'd been forced to resort to more elaborate methods of murder. It had been mildly amusing watching those people fight to stay alive for as long as they could, but it didn't beat a clean, simple slice through the carotid artery. Or expertly maneuver the knife between the ribs so you got a clear shot at the heart. Or if you were feeling particularly malicious, you could go with a nice, deep gut wound and watch the person die a long, slow, and painful death.

He snorted at the memories of when he had done just that to anyone who had gotten in his way.

Hunter wasn't a good man.

He wasn't even an okay man.

His life had been hard. A drunk father who preferred to use his fists rather than his voice, a mother who was too busy working four jobs to pay the bills to be around. Young Hunter hadn't been interested in school, he didn't want to work hard and find a way out of the environment life had thrown him into. Gangs ruled his poverty-stricken neighborhood, one in particular dominated.

The Devil's Snakes.

Joining the gang at the ripe old age of eight, he'd paid his dues, proved he was a cold-hearted monster who would do whatever was asked of him, and had climbed in the ranks. Dealing in drugs and women, the motorcycle club had earned him more money than he could ever have hoped to make if he'd studied hard in school, gone to college, and gotten a job.

Anything he wanted, he bought.

Money got you anything you wanted.

Almost.

Unfortunately, the one thing Hunter wanted the most he couldn't buy.

At least not in the regular sense of the word.

He might not be able to purchase what he wanted with cold, hard cash, but he could exact a different sort of payment.

A payment in blood.

Groaning behind him told him that his time to collect was almost here, and after over a year of waiting, it was hard to believe that this moment was upon him. He had dreamed about this, about how he'd feel, about how good it would be to exact his revenge.

"Wakey, wakey, *Spike Boris.*" He sneered at the man he had trussed up in the corner of the kitchen.

The man grunted, groaned again, then snapped awake with the ease of someone who was well practiced at being in control of any and every situation they found themselves in.

Unlucky for him, this time Hunter was the one with the control.

A pair of cold hazel eyes stared at him, and although he knew the drugs he'd used to incapacitate the other man were still in his system, the gaze was clear and focused.

"Leaving the window open was a mistake." Hunter grinned. "I didn't know how I would get inside, but you made it so easy."

Assessing eyes took in the plastic zip ties that bound his ankles and he wriggled his hands, which were bound behind his back. Hunter could tell the second his gaze landed on the unconscious woman shackled to the floor.

If it was possible for smoke to come out of someone's ears and for them to breathe fire then that was exactly what the man he now knew was called Will Black was doing.

"Should we wake her up?" he goaded, pushing back from the table and walking to the sink where he had earlier set a glass in case one or both of his victims needed a little help regaining consciousness.

"You hurt her, I'll kill you," Will growled low in his throat.

Hunter laughed. "I'd like to see you try." He turned on the tap and held the glass under the faucet, waiting while it filled with cold water before shutting it off. Then he walked over to where he'd left Renee Miller. Her ankles were fixed to the floor with metal cuffs he had attached to the hardwood floors, as was one of her wrists. The other was free because he couldn't put her in position until she'd woken up.

"You don't know who you're dealing with," Will said. Despite the fact that he was leaning propped against the wall, and although he appeared relaxed, tension was coiled up in each and every one of his muscles like he was ready to pounce at a moment's notice.

"No," Hunter growled back. "It's *you* who doesn't know who you're dealing with. Do you have any idea how many men just like you I've killed?"

"Any idea how many men *I've* killed?" Will shot back.

"I know of one you've killed." Hunter met the man's gaze squarely. Will hadn't asked who he was or what he was doing here, nor had he asked what he would do to himself and Renee. There was no need to. Will Black knew exactly who he was.

"He deserved what he got."

Anger coursed through him. "He was my brother," he hissed.

"He was a rapist. He broke into my house and raped my woman, Rafe got what he deserved. In fact he got a lot less." Will maintained eye contact and didn't appear to be concerned that he and the woman he claimed to love were about to die.

"Now you and your woman are going to get what you deserved." Will Black had infiltrated the Devil's Snakes, managed to figure out that Rafe was the one who had raped Renee, and then killed him. It hadn't taken him long to figure out that Spike Boris didn't exist and was merely an alias for an undercover cop. "It was almost too easy," he said as he stood above Renee. "All I had to do was follow her, and I knew sooner or later that she'd lead me right to you."

"Is that how you found out about Josiah?"

"I saw the man at her work, recognized him, didn't take a genius to figure out that if I started killing people in the same sort of way he did that you'd be looking for him and not me. He followed her here too, only I got to him before he could do anything more than check into a hotel room. Aren't you glad I stabbed him and kept him in the trunk of my car so he couldn't touch your woman?" Hunter goaded, enjoying every second of this.

"Killing us won't bring your brother back."

"No, but it will make me feel a whole lot better." Rafe was his little brother, he'd been looking after him since they were small boys. He'd taken beatings from their father so Rafe hadn't had to, he'd found them a new family when their own didn't care about what happened to them, and he'd get revenge for his brother's murder even if it wouldn't bring Rafe back.

Tossing the water in the glass on the woman at his feet had the desired effect, and she began to stir. It didn't take long for her to figure out what was going on, and she thrashed against the metal bands at her ankles and left wrist.

"Will?" she cried out.

"Here, Little Bird, everything's going to be okay."

"Aww, Little Bird, how sweet," he sneered. "Although how you think everything is going to be okay is beyond me."

When he crouched at Renee's side she shrunk away from him, large dark eyes wide with fear. "Who are you?"

"That's right we weren't formally introduced the other night, you busy taking a swim. I'm Hunter Ford, I believe you knew my brother," he sneered.

Renee gasped. Her entire body trembled, and she tried to squirm away from him, freezing when she spied the knife. He'd embedded it in the floor between the two wrist shackles and would position her above it in a pushup pose. When her arms could no longer hold up her weight, the knife would pierce her chest, killing her.

"A two for one," he smiled at her. "Your man gets to watch you die, knowing he's powerless to save you, and then I'll kill him."

"Let Renee go. She doesn't have anything to do with this. She's not the one who killed your brother."

"No, Will," Renee gasped.

"Don't worry." Hunter reached out and ruffled her hair. "You won't have to live without him. Neither of you are leaving this room alive."

With that, he grabbed Renee's free wrist, and although she tried to fight him off, she was already bound and still woozy from the drugs, and he was easily able to pull her up so her shackled arm was straight and maneuver her into position.

"Will," she wept as tears streamed down her face, "I love you."

"I love you too, honey. Just hold on okay, trust me, I promised you I wouldn't ever let you down again, and that's a promise I don't intend to break."

"What sweet words," he mocked as he snapped the metal cuff around Renee's right wrist. "Too bad it's a promise you won't be keeping."

Hunter knew about broken promises.

When he was six and Rafe four, he'd promised his little brother that he would always look out for him, that he'd slay any dragons who came along whether they be their drunk father, social workers, or undercover cops.

He'd failed.

Will Black had done the unthinkable, infiltrated the infamous motorcycle club to find which of their members had been the perpetrator in his woman's assault. He'd somehow found the answers he'd needed and delivered his own form of justice.

Well, now it was time for him to get justice.

Revenge would be a balm to soothe his raging fury. Blood would flow in this room tonight, and in the morning he would be free of the shackles of guilt over not protecting his brother.

3:12 A.M.

Every muscle in his body was tense and ready for action.

If Hunter Ford thought he was walking out of this room alive, then he was sorely mistaken.

Will was simply waiting for his opportunity, and then he would strike. If he was here alone he would already have made his move, but he had Renee's safety to consider so he had to think things through.

He was restrained, but the simple zip ties weren't anything that he couldn't break through in a manner of seconds. Too bad for Hunter he didn't know he was dealing with a former SEAL. Once he was free, he'd make sure Hunter met the same fate his brother had.

Ignoring the lingering effects of whatever drugs Hunter had given them, he watched as the other man grabbed Renee and began to drag her up, above the knife he had somehow embedded in the floor, blade up.

"Will," Renee cried, "I love you."

"I love you too, honey. Just hold on okay, trust me, I promised you I wouldn't ever let you down again, and that's a promise I don't intend to break." Wriggling away from the wall, he lifted his bound hand up, leaned forward a little and brought them down hard against his back. It took only two tries before the plastic snapped.

"What sweet words," Hunter mocked him as he snapped the metal cuff around Renee's right wrist. "Too bad it's a promise you won't be keeping."

Too bad for Hunter he hadn't done his homework.

Ignoring his bound ankles, he rolled and collided with Hunter, knocking the man over before he'd even noticed that his prisoner was no longer bound and idly awaiting his fate.

Hunter growled as his head slammed into the floor.

Using momentum and the element of surprise, Will was able to pin the man beneath him, ignoring the way the plastic zip tie cut into his flesh as he planted his knees on either side of Hunter's hips.

Satisfaction screamed through his knuckles and up to his shoulder as his fist connected with Hunter's jaw. This man had no right to stalk Renee, follow her here, kill people, and all just to get to him. Hunter's brother Rafe had broken into their home, raped Renee, traumatized her, and started the chain of events that led to them separating. The man had deserved death. How many other women had he assaulted? How many more would he have assaulted if he was still alive?

Will swung again, but this time Hunter blocked the blow and swung his own fist, slamming it into the side of his head.

The blow to the head combined with the drugs was enough to knock him off balance, sending him sprawling onto the kitchen floor.

"You killed Rafe, you deserve to die," Hunter screamed.

"Will, look out, he has a knife," Renee shrieked.

Taking Renee's warning as seriously as he would any member of his SEAL team or any partner he'd ever worked with, he rolled to the side just as Hunter made his move and missed being sliced open by mere seconds.

Continuing through with the roll until he was on his back he kicked out with his bound feet, connecting squarely with Hunter's chest. The man grunted, then stumbled backward, the knife falling from his hand and clattering onto the floor as he collided with the counter.

Pushing up onto his feet, it took Will a second to regain his balance and Hunter used that split second to utter a growl that was more animal than human, and with black eyes that glittered with pure, undiluted rage, Hunter launched.

Will pivoted, and it gave him enough of a buffer that when they fell in a tangle of limbs the other man didn't land on top of him. Hunter got in another couple of blows, one to the side of his head and another to his jaw, but Will took the blows, his focus elsewhere.

"Will, I can't hold on much longer," Renee's panicked voice joined the grunts of their brawl.

Positioned as she was above the knife, she wasn't able to move backward or sideways without the blade cutting her. Even without the drugs in her system that had knocked them out, she wouldn't have been able to hold the straight-armed pushup position for long.

Her fear, which was a palpable thing that he could feel as surely as he could feel his own anger, was enough to spur him on and his fingers curled around the knife that Hunter had dropped.

Pain spiraled through his head as Hunter got in a good punch right to his cheek, a blow he was sure had broken the bone, and he fought not to pass out, if he did, not only was he as good as dead but Renee was too, and he had promised her that he wouldn't let anyone hurt her ever again.

That was a promise he intended to keep.

Lifting the knife, he plunged it deep into the other man's back on his left side.

From the wheezing and gurgling and the way Hunter slumped against him, he knew he'd hit his target and pierced the man's heart.

Warm blood coated his bare skin, and he had to force his now heavy limbs to function. Hunter had gotten in at least four or five good shots, and he'd be surprised if he didn't have a concussion and a broken cheekbone.

"Will," Renee whimpered, "I can't hold on." Her pained moan shot straight through him, more powerful than any blow Hunter could have delivered.

"Hold on, baby, I'm coming." Mustering strength his drugged and battered body was lacking, he shoved the dying body of the man who had tormented River's End for the last week off him and staggered to his feet. Pulling the knife out of Hunter's body, he used it to cut through the zip ties binding his ankles and then dropped down at Renee's side.

Blood dripped from her shoulder where she had obviously tried to lean slightly to the side so the blade of the knife punctured her shoulder and not her chest above her heart. Her arms trembled with the exertion of holding up her body, no doubt strengthened only by the knowledge that if she let go she was dead.

"It's okay, Little Bird, I'm here," he soothed, running a hand over her tangled locks.

"You're hurt," she whispered, twisting her head to look up at him.

"I'm fine," he assured her.

"My arms are going to give out," she told him.

Wrapping an arm around her waist, Will said, "Let me take your weight."

"He hurt you," she said, stubbornly fighting him.

"Really, honey, I'm okay. Now just relax, let go, let me take your weight." When she didn't comply, he added, "Trust me, Renee. I won't let anything happen to you."

Slowly, carefully, tentatively, Renee relaxed, allowing him to take her weight. She was small, and he really wasn't badly injured, he was easily able to support her.

"See, told you," he teased.

She huffed a small chuckle. "Now what? You can't just sit there and hold me up until someone finds us here."

"You doubting me, Little Bird?"

"No, never, you always have something up your sleeve." He could hear the smile in her voice even though he couldn't see her face, and was proud of her for holding it together as well as she had.

"Hunter has to have a key for the locks."

"He's the brother of the man who ...?"

"Yeah, he is."

"You knew him when you were undercover?"

"Yes. He's not a good man, Renee, don't feel bad for him. He and his motorcycle club deal in drugs and women. They kill anyone who gets in their way, innocent or not. Rafe deserved to die for what he did to you, and Hunter was going to kill us. It was him or us, and no way was I letting him kill you."

"I'm not angry, Will," she said softly, tilting her head so her face brushed against his shoulder. "You saved our lives. Thank you."

"You never have to thank me for protecting you." Leaning down, he kissed her cheek, then supporting Renee's weight with one arm, he reached over and snagged a hold of Hunter's jeans, dragging the man closer so he could rifle through his pockets in search of the key. "Got it," he announced triumphantly when he found it. "Just a moment more, honey. You're going to have to hold yourself up again so I can get you unlocked."

"I can do that," she assured him confidently.

A little less sure than she was, Will slowly released his hold on her, making sure that she had enough strength to keep herself upright before he completely released her and moved around so he was in front of her. Making quick work of the locks he freed both her hands and then helped her move sideways so she could lie on the floor.

Shuffling on his knees down to the end of her body, he unlocked the metal cuffs securing her ankles, and then finally she was free.

Standing, he grabbed a dishtowel from the oven door and then crouched beside Renee, pressing it to the wound on her shoulder. "I don't know how deep it is but keep pressure on it," he said as he picked up one of her hands and held it to the towel. Then he scooped her into his arms and carried her outside, picking up his phone from the table near the door on the way.

Outside in the warm early summer morning, he sank onto the front stoop and settled Renee in his lap as he called Abe to let him know what had happened and that they'd need an ambulance, the coroner, and CSU all sent to his house.

Calls made, he tucked Renee's head under his chin and covered her hand with his, pressing the towel against her wound to stem the flow of blood.

He'd nearly gotten them both killed.

Hunter Ford had latched onto Renee because he'd figured out that his brother's death circled back to her rape. Rafe hadn't been shy about bragging about what he'd done to her and at least a dozen other women that Will knew about. That was how he'd known which member of the Devil's Snakes had committed the assault.

If he hadn't made the choice to go after Renee's rapist for revenge then not only would he have been there for her when she'd needed him as she recovered and dealt with the emotional fallout, but she wouldn't have nearly died twice in the last week.

Because of him, she'd had to fight to stay afloat in the pool at her mother's house for hours while she waited for someone to find her.

Because of him, she'd been drugged and chained up, forced to hold herself up or get a knife through her heart.

His choices had hurt her over and over again.

Will had promised her that he would fight for her—for them—but he had also promised her that he would never again cause her pain, and yet he was starting to realize that no matter what he did, he *did* end up causing her pain.

The woman he held in his arms was the most precious thing in his life, the only woman he would ever love, but did he love her enough to walk away so he could never hurt her again?

∼

12:26 P.M.

Where was Will?

Something was wrong.

Renee knew that without him having to say it.

Ever since the cops and paramedics had shown up at his house, Will had been distant, and she could feel him withdrawing. She had no idea why or what had precipitated it. They'd spent a wonderful night together. He'd been sweet and gentle with her when she'd woken from a nightmare, he'd been about to make love to her when that man had come in through the window and shot them with some sort of drugged darts. He'd saved her life, soothing and reassuring her when she'd felt like things were hopeless, and her arms would give out at any second sending the knife which was just an inch or two below her chest when her arms were straight, slicing into her heart.

Then nothing.

He'd been distant and borderline cold.

When Abe and the others had arrived, he had passed her off to his brother, telling her that they both had to give a statement and that it was better if they weren't together again until they had so that no defense attorney could say they had conspired and cooked up a story to explain Hunter Ford's death.

But Will wouldn't be charged with his death.

The man had stalked her, followed her here, killed several people, tried to kill her once before, then broken in and tried to kill her and Will. They both had the injuries to prove what had happened. Will had killed Hunter because it was the only way that the two of them could live. No one would press charges against him for that.

If it wasn't worry about being charged with Hunter's murder, then maybe he was more seriously hurt than he'd led her to believe and he just didn't want her to know. She wasn't sure he was though because he'd been able to hold up her weight while simultaneously searching for the key to unlock her shackles, and then he'd carried her from the house.

So if he wasn't afraid of being arrested, and wasn't seriously hurt, why was he pushing her away?

She was giving herself a headache worrying over this.

Renee rubbed at her temples and then pushed herself into a sitting position—wincing at the pain in her shoulder where the knife had cut her—and swung her legs over the side of the bed. She needed some fresh air.

The emergency room was quiet, Julian was supposed to be keeping an eye on her, but he was off to the side with his cousin Levi, who had treated her and told her she could leave later in the day, once the drugs Hunter had given them were completely out of her system.

Sneaking past them, she made her way to the door and stepped through it, out into the heat. The feel of the sun on her skin and the gentle breeze ruffling her loose locks immediately went a long way to clearing away the tightness in her head.

Until she turned and caught sight of Will walking toward his car.

He was leaving?

Without even coming to see her?

Anger took hold inside her. He'd been the one to pursue her when he learned she was back in town, not the other way around. He'd told her that he loved her, that he'd made a mistake in leaving her, and that he regretted it. He'd said that he would never let her down again, that he would fight for her and earn her trust back.

He'd told her all of that, and yet here he was sneaking away and leaving her behind.

Again.

Before she even registered what she was doing, she was storming across the parking lot. "Going somewhere?" she demanded, her voice dripping with sarcasm. She wasn't usually a sarcastic person, but right now she was fuming. She'd been a fool to give Will Black a second chance.

Will spun around to face her, the guilty look on his face confirming her suspicions that he had indeed been intending to leave without so much as a goodbye.

"Umm," he mumbled, "I thought you were ... resting."

"You couldn't have waited?"

He sighed, and the fact that he didn't look happy with what he was about to say made her stomach drop. "Look, Renee, maybe you were right. Maybe we should have left the past in the past. We had both moved on with our lives, trying to get back what we lost was probably a bit naïve."

"What?" she asked incredulously.

"I hurt you, baby, again." The raw pain in his voice was mirrored in his face. This was killing him, but he would walk away anyway because he was so determined that he knew what was best for her.

"Tell me you're joking."

"Hunter Ford nearly killed you because of me. Because I couldn't not go after the man who hurt you. I killed his brother, and he was here to get his revenge. He nearly succeeded." He reached out and lightly touched his fingers to the bandage Levi had put on her shoulder. The wound hadn't even been deep enough to need stitches, it was hardly cause to tear down what they were rebuilding.

"You have quite the ego don't you?" she quipped.

"What?" His brow crinkled in confusion.

"You are so pigheaded, you refuse to even entertain the possibility that you might be wrong. You keep deciding what I want—what's best for me—without even asking me. You left last time because you decided what I needed was to know that the man who hurt me was dead or in prison. And now you're walking away again because you've decided that you're a danger to me and if you hang around I'll get hurt again. Well you know what, mister?" She poked a finger into his chest and craned her head up so she could meet his eye. "I'm not going anywhere. I quit my job, I'm moving back to River's End, I don't know what I'm going to do yet, but whatever it is I'll be doing it here. I'm going to Maggie's hotel, I'll text you the room number once I'm checked in. When you're ready to apologize and admit that *you're* the one who keeps running scared, I'll be there waiting for you."

With that, Renee stood on tiptoe so she could kiss him then she turned and walked away.

This time she wasn't giving up what she wanted without a fight.

Sixteen months ago, when Will had turned up on her doorstep to tell her that her attacker was no longer a threat, her emotions had been too raw, she'd been too hurt to even consider giving him—them—a second chance.

But not this time.

She'd fought through too much, she'd worked too hard to rebuild her life, and she'd worked too hard to let her guard down and let Will back in to slam that barrier back up.

If Will didn't want to fight for them then she would. She wasn't letting the Ford brothers take anything else from her.

It took about an hour because Julian had to go to Will's house to get her purse and cell phone, but once she had them, she called a cab and went to the Honeysuckle Hotel. Maggie checked her in, and by the time she reached her room she was exhausted.

Shedding her clothes, she walked straight into the bathroom, turned the shower on as hot as she could stand, and once the room was full of steam she stepped under the spray.

The hot water went a long way toward relaxing her, and by the time she stepped out, she felt mostly human. Renee carefully dried the wound on her shoulder and applied another bandage then realized that she didn't have any clothes bar the hospital scrubs Levi had given her.

Too tired to care, she walked naked out of the bathroom and headed for the bed when there was a sharp knock on her door.

She didn't even have to open it to know who was on the other side.

When she threw open the door and Will saw her standing before him naked, he uttered a low groan then stalked inside her room, slamming and locking the door behind him, and advanced on her.

"You came," she said breathily, barely able to think when he looked at her like that.

"You were right, I was being a coward." He was breathing heavily, but his hand was gentle when it reached out and tenderly caressed her cheek. "You're an intelligent woman, and you deserve someone who listens to you and doesn't make decisions for you."

"I want you, Will. I want us. But I don't want to spend the rest of my life worrying that when things get tough you'll decide I'm better off without you and you'll leave again. I can't live like that, and it's not fair to ask me to." As much as she loved him and it would kill her to walk away, she wasn't stupid, and if he couldn't offer stability then she was better off alone than with him.

"I'm not asking you to, honey. I'll be the man you need me to be because the alternative is hurting you again, and that's something I won't do."

The look in his eyes told her he was serious and that was all she needed to know.

Being raped didn't have to steal her future, she and Will could have everything they'd talked about since they were teenagers.

"Kiss me now, Will," she whispered.

Pouncing on her like he was starving and she was the most delicious meal, he wrapped an arm around her waist and yanked her up against his hard body. His lips crashed to hers and he kissed her. His mouth feasted on her as he backed her up until her calves bumped against the bed, then he laid her down on it.

She was already naked, and it didn't take him long to strip out of his t-shirt and denim shorts.

All he'd done was kiss her, and already her body felt like it was seconds away from combusting. While his lips consumed her his hands roved over her body, touching her breasts, teasing her between her legs, and by the time she felt him prodding at her entrance she was balanced right on the edge.

Then in a second, her worst nightmare came true.

It wasn't Will about to enter her body, it was her rapist.

It wasn't Maggie's hotel where she was sprawled on the bed, it was the house where she and Will used to live.

She wasn't about to make love to the man she adored, she was about to be raped by a stranger.

Like a switch had been flipped she cried out, shoving at the large body pressing her into the mattress. She fought like her life—her soul—depended on it. She couldn't see, couldn't hear, couldn't process anything but the thick dark cloud that surrounded her.

The next cognizant realization she had was that she was wrapped in a strong pair of arms, tucked against a warm body, being rocked gently from side to side as lips touched her temple in a string of soft kisses.

Humiliation burned brightly inside her.

Not only had she just made a fool out of herself by freaking out in the middle of sex, but she was afraid that Will would decide that him coming here was a bad idea because he'd triggered a flashback and thus hurt her.

Just when she thought the worst was behind her and it would be smooth sailing from here on out, she was proved wrong.

Tears blurred her vision as she lifted her head to meet Will's gaze, terrified of what she was going to see in it.

~

3:33 P.M.

The shame and uncertainty in Renee's eyes kicked him in the gut.

Will hated that it was there because of him.

He didn't want that, he didn't want her to always be wary around him, always waiting for him to decide that he knew what was best for her and walk away again.

That was something he would never do.

He was done being a coward.

Renee was right, he'd run because *he* couldn't deal with what had happened to her. It was easier to focus on revenge, on giving her closure, than it was to be there and hold her when she cried, listen to her screams as nightmares stalked her dreams, to watch her fall apart as she struggled to cope with and process being a victim of sexual assault.

But his girl hadn't fallen apart.

She was stronger than he could ever hope to be. She had fought every day for the last two years to get her life back, and she had succeeded. She excelled at her job, she cared for her family even though they were difficult, and she had given him a second—and a third—chance even though he didn't deserve it.

He could only hope to be as strong as Renee one day.

From here on out, he wasn't running when things were tough, when his fears of hurting Renee, of not being enough for her, urged him to tuck tail and run he would fight through it. If Renee could deal with what had happened to her, then he could as well. As much as the very notion of someone violating the woman he loved made him want to rip his own skin off just to eliminate the pain, he had to accept it had happened and find a way to cope.

He couldn't live in denial forever.

Renee's small hands lifted to rest on his chest, and she pushed, trying to get him to let her go, and he realized he had been lost in thought and hadn't addressed her freak out.

"Let me go, Will," she said quietly, steadfastly avoiding meeting his eye.

"No." He tightened his hold on her.

"This is embarrassing enough, let me go. Please." Her voice wobbled on that last word, and once again he hated himself for causing her pain.

"There's nothing to be embarrassed about," he assured her, tucking her under his chin, cradling her head in his hand, and touching his lips to her temple.

"I freaked out in the middle of sex," she said dubiously.

"After what you've been through I don't think that's anything unnatural."

"I didn't when we slept together before, and it's been two years, I should be over it by now." Her voice was full of self-recrimination like she believed there was something wrong with her. That mode of thinking he was squashing before it took hold.

"Everything that happened with Hunter probably brought it all back up. It doesn't matter, Renee. I mean, I hate that you had a flash-back, it makes me want to kill Rafe Ford all over again, but it doesn't matter. We'll have sex again when you're ready, if that's tonight, great, if it's next week, or next month, or next year, that's fine. Honey, I love you, I'm here for you, I know you have psychological scars from what happened, and this time I'll be here to support you while you work through things. I'm sorry I was a coward, that I couldn't deal with things and left you, but you've given me another chance, and I won't ever let you down again."

"You said that last time," Renee reminded him.

"But now I know I'll lose you if I let you down again." Guilt for nearly getting Renee killed had him pushing her away this morning, but when Renee confronted him in the hospital parking lot, he realized that if he persisted in beating himself up because he hadn't prevented her from being raped, and because he hadn't prevented Hunter from coming after her, he would lose her.

For real this time.

Renee's trust in him was still shaky, and if he broke it now she'd never give him another chance.

"I love you, Will. And I want to be with you. But ..." she trailed off, dragged in a breath, then continued, "if you ever push me away again things will be over between us."

"I know, baby." Lifting her up, he stood then set her down on the bed, crossing to his clothes to get something from his shorts pocket. There was a reason he hadn't come straight here from the hospital, there was something he'd needed to do first, something that couldn't wait. He'd intended to talk to her about it as soon as he arrived, but then she'd opened the door naked, and he couldn't not look at her glorious body and not make love to it.

"What are you doing?" Renee asked suspiciously.

"What I should have done a long time ago." Down on one knee, he took Renee's left hand in his and held out the ring in its small black velvet box. "I put my job before you, thinking that you'd always be there waiting for me when I came home. And you were. I took you for granted, and then I abandoned you when you needed me the most because I was afraid I would let you down again. You are more than I deserve, and yet here you are willing to give me another chance. You are the most amazing woman, smart, beautiful, kind, and the strongest woman—person—I have ever met. I love you, Little Bird, and I vow right here and now to make you the number one priority in my life. I will love you, and worship you, and cherish you every day for the rest of my life. Renee, will you bless me by giving me what I don't deserve but am asking for anyway by agreeing to be my wife?"

Renee stared at him wide-eyed like she couldn't believe he was really saying this. "Did you buy a ring on the way here?"

"No, I've had this ring for two years. After I told you that Rafe Ford was no longer a threat and you said things were over between us, I drove back here. Abe eventually found me by the river and offered me a job, I went to throw the ring in the water, thinking that I had lost you for good, but I couldn't. Maybe it was the universe telling me that it wasn't over, that one day we would find our way back to each other. I took the ring home, kept it in my nightstand."

Renee reached out to touch her fingertips to his cheek, tracing just underneath the row of stitches his cousin Levi had put in to close the gash there. "You, me together, that's all I ever wanted. I'm so glad you kept the ring."

"Is that a yes?" he asked a little nervously. The idea that Renee would say no had never occurred to him, but the fact that she still hadn't actually accepted his marriage proposal was making him anxious.

She giggled and then threw her arms around his neck. "Of course it's a yes! We still have lots we need to work on before we're back to where we were before, but I want to be with you, I want to marry you, I want to have children, and the future we've been talking about since we were teenagers. I love you, Will Black." She kissed him, all traces of her earlier anxiety about freaking out gone, as she dragged him closer.

"Hold on, Little Bird," he said, hands on her shoulders as he gently eased her back. "I have to put the ring on."

Renee held out her hand, and he slipped the ring onto her finger. "It's gorgeous, Will. It must have cost you a fortune. Are those pink diamonds?"

"Yep, I know they're your favorite." The ring had cost a fortune, not that he would tell her that, he'd chosen it because as soon as he saw it he could imagine it on Renee's slender finger. That was all he needed to know. The smile on her face now made it worth every penny, and being able to look at that smile every day for the rest of his life was his idea of paradise.

It had been a long road to get to this point, a long, bumpy road, but now that they were here all of the heartache and turmoil faded away. The past would always be a part of their journey, there were mistakes they had to learn from so they didn't repeat them, but for the first time in two long years, the future was brighter than the past.

"Are you going to make love to me now?" Renee asked, her hands running across his bare chest.

"Are you sure?" As much as he wanted to bury himself inside her, he'd meant it when he said that it didn't matter how long it took her to be ready.

"Are you going to tell me you know better if I say I'm sure?" She arched a challenging brow, silently daring him to back up his claims that he wasn't going to make decisions for her again and instead listen to her and believe that she knew what was best for her and what she wanted.

"I learned my lesson, Little Bird," he promised as he laid her back against the mattress and kissed her.

Return to River's End as Julian Black fights to get back the woman he loves after walking away from her once already in the seventh story in this gripping, emotionally charged romantic suspense series!

Some Trust Can Be Rebuilt (River's End Rescues #7).

Also by Jane Blythe

CRUSHED RUBY

FRACTURED DIAMOND

SHATTERED AMETHYST

SPLINTERED EMERALD

SALVAGING MARIGOLD

River's End Rescues Series

COCKY SAVIOR

SOME REGRETS ARE FOREVER

SOME FEARS CAN CONTROL YOU

SOME LIES WILL HAUNT YOU

SOME QUESTIONS HAVE NO ANSWERS

SOME TRUTH CAN BE DISTORTED

SOME TRUST CAN BE REBUILT

SOME MISTAKES ARE UNFORGIVABLE

Candella Sisters' Heroes Series

LITTLE DOLLS

LITTLE HEARTS

LITTLE BALLERINA

Storybook Murders Series

NURSERY RHYME KILLER

FAIRYTALE KILLER

FABLE KILLER

Saving SEALs Series

SAVING RYDER
SAVING ERIC
SAVING OWEN
SAVING LOGAN
SAVING GRAYSON
SAVING CHARLIE

Prey Security Series

PROTECTING EAGLE
PROTECTING RAVEN
PROTECTING FALCON
PROTECTING SPARROW
PROTECTING HAWK
PROTECTING DOVE

Prey Security: Alpha Team Series

DEADLY RISK
LETHAL RISK
EXTREME RISK
FATAL RISK
COVERT RISK
SAVAGE RISK

Prey Security: Artemis Team Series

IVORY'S FIGHT

PEARL'S FIGHT

LACEY'S FIGHT

OPAL'S FIGHT

Prey Security: Bravo Team Series

VICIOUS SCARS

RUTHLESS SCARS

Christmas Romantic Suspense Series

CHRISTMAS HOSTAGE

CHRISTMAS CAPTIVE

CHRISTMAS VICTIM

YULETIDE PROTECTOR

YULETIDE GUARD

YULETIDE HERO

HOLIDAY GRIEF

Conquering Fear Series (Co-written with Amanda Siegrist)

DROWNING IN YOU

OUT OF THE DARKNESS

CLOSING IN

About the Author

USA Today bestselling author Jane Blythe writes action-packed romantic suspense and military romance featuring protective heroes and heroines who are survivors. One of Jane's most popular series includes Prey Security, part of Susan Stoker's OPERATION ALPHA world! Writing in that world alongside authors such as Janie Crouch and Riley Edwards has been a blast, and she looks forward to bringing more books to this genre, both within and outside of Stoker's world. When Jane isn't binge-reading she's counting down to Christmas and adding to her 200+ teddy bear collection!

To connect and keep up to date please visit any of the following

Printed in Great Britain
by Amazon

48206683R00119